ABOUT THIS BOOK

With her future already fated by others, vampire hybrid Elle makes the most of her present—but a friend's betrayal could end it all.

Seventeen-year-old vampire-dryad hybrid Elle can't live up to her parents' expectations. She's snubbed by her dad's bloodline-obsessed vampire family while her mom's dryad side has determined her fate—to return to New York City and protect Central Park.

Unsure of her place in the world yet held to promises her family made, Elle dreads leaving her friends as well as breaking things off with her wolf-shifter boyfriend, Kase. With her destiny out of her hands, Elle is determined to control what she can.

Even though Kase Kasun has spent his life living in the shadows of his family name and the weight it carries, he's embraced his role as a protector of Havenwood Falls. Everything had been worked out, until Elle started distancing herself. Kase knows the space she's creating between them will only make room for trouble.

Intent on savoring every last minute together, Elle, Kase, and all their friends plan an epic spring break camping trip. But when one of Elle's so-called friends turns out to be an enemy intent on taking her out of Havenwood Falls, her life may come to an untimely end. Promises are made to be broken, and only the moon has the power to save her now.

HAVENWOOD FALLS HIGH BOOKS

Written in the Stars by Kallie Ross

Reawakened by Morgan Wylie

The Fall by Kristen Yard

Somewhere Within by Amy Hale

Awaken the Soul by Michele G. Miller

Bound by Shadows by Cameo Renae

Fata Morgana by E.J. Fechenda

Forever Emeline by Katie M. John

Reclamation by AnnaLisa Grant

Avenoir by Daniele Lanzarotta

Avenge the Heart by Michele G. Miller

Curse the Night by R.K. Ryals

Blood & Iron by Amy Hale

Shadows & Spells by Cameo Renae

Falling Deep by J.L. Weil

Saving Infiniti by Rose Garcia

Willful by Liz Ferry

Cast in Moonlight by Ali Winters

Promise the Moon by Kallie Ross

Blurred Lines by Daniele Lanzarotta

Ascending Darkness by J.L. Weil

Finding Infiniti by Rose Garcia

Unicorn's Lament by Megan Linski

Paper Bird by Amy Richie

Predestined by Valia Lind

Rediscovered by Morgan Wylie

Ashes of Fate by Apryl Baker

Stay up to date at www.HavenwoodFalls.com

ALSO BY KALLIE ROSS

Defying Gravity: A Havenwood Falls Novella

Written in the Stars: A Havenwood Falls High Novella

A Pack of Lies: A Legends of Havenwood Falls Novella

Descent: A Lost Tribe (Book 1)

Defend: A Lost Tribe (Book 2)

Evelyn: A Cupid Chronicles Novella

Unbreakable: The Cupid Chronicles

PROMISE THE MOON

A HAVENWOOD FALLS HIGH NOVELLA

KALLIE ROSS

Dedicated to Morgan.
The accountability and encouragement you've given me over the years has meant the world. Thank you!

CHAPTER 1

ELLE

The Havenwood Falls High bell rang sharply, alerting me to the end of the school day. Finally, spring break. Lifting my head from the pages of my assigned reading, *A Tale of Two Cities*, I watched the rest of the class hustle toward the hallway. Normally, I loved losing myself in a good book, but even with two years of French, I had a hard time keeping up with Darnay and the Defarges.

The thick novel didn't fit in my backpack, so I secured the tattered paperback in my coat pocket, shouldered my bag, and made my way to my locker. There was no need to carry thirty pounds of books, since I'd only need one of them to complete my homework. The weight didn't bother me, because I had super strength. Being a vampire half-breed had perks; for example, I didn't have to deal with bloodlust like my father did. Dryad blood pumped through my veins, powerful enough to subdue any unbecoming urges a young vampire would have. Only problem was each half-breed benefit came with inconveniences, like being able to hear every thought from every mind in the building. Over the last year, with the help of my parents, friends, and night classes at the Academy, I'd mostly learned to control each of my abilities, including the ones I hadn't expected.

The school's hallways always buzzed with the latest gossip and hormones. Tuning out self-conscious teenagers had become second nature. Disregarding arrogant and even lustful thoughts took a little more concentration. And the weirdest part of mind reading wasn't all the jumbled thoughts, but it was seeing them in my mind's eye. My ability was similar to reading a book and visualizing the story like a movie.

So when I heard Ana Novak's thoughts about Kase Kasun, I not only caught a few details about what a good kisser he was, but I envisioned Kase's lips so close I could feel his warm breath brush over my cheek.

I pressed my palm to my forehead to clear my thoughts.

When I looked up, the two were at the end of the corridor across from my locker. Ana was leaning against the old blue-painted metal facing Kase, and she grinned up at him and giggled. Then, as if she sensed I was watching, she nudged his shoulder playfully. Her touch lingered a second too long. He glanced down at the spot she'd touched and shook his head. Her bottom lip pouted out flirtatiously, and he ignored her attempt to win him back and turned to walk in my direction without a word.

As his eyes met mine, he frowned. We'd both been trying to ignore the spectacle Ana made of herself on a daily basis, but somehow she'd found out I called things off romantically with Kase during the holiday break. Ever since, I'd been trying to avoid both of them. Kase had known from the beginning, since his split with Ana, that I wasn't staying. My family had always expected me to move back to New York after graduation. Not to mention, I'd die if I didn't bond with a tree in Central Park by my next birthday. After I'd gained control of my strange powers, and the rumors about the mysterious death of my ex-boyfriend were replaced by who wore what at the latest gala, I'd had to beg my parents to allow me to stay in Havenwood Falls to graduate. Neither of my parents were biological, but they'd been looking after me since the night they found me. I'd been no more than a few months old, and I'd been laid at the foot of my mother's tree in the park.

Kase and I had agreed to stay friends after the holidays, but seeing him through Ana's thoughts made me want to vomit. Every day, the love I felt for Kase grew heavier in my chest. For the last few months, when I knew he had a class in one hallway, I'd go down another so I wouldn't have to face him. Lugging love around, instead of giving it to Kase, made me realize sadness isn't a void. True sorrow is a weight.

Behind him, Ana gave me a death glare. I shrugged and turned toward the exit. Avoiding Ana had become essential for both of us. She had a way of making me crazy, and I couldn't risk losing control in a school filled with humans who didn't know about our supernatural world.

Thirty pounds wasn't that heavy anyway.

Kase walked faster to catch up with me, and I could feel him getting closer. Eluding him had been impossible. The warmth he radiated had to be because he was a wolf shifter; at least, that's what I'd convinced myself. It couldn't be anything more. We couldn't be anything more than friends. It would be easier the next time I saw him. The truth was I'd be seeing him more this next week than I'd allowed myself for months.

Kase cleared his throat, and when I looked over at him, one corner of his mouth pulled up, revealing a dimple.

"You have mean girl cooties," I teased, and wrinkled my nose when he tried to hold my hand—again. It was partially my fault he kept trying. The few times we found ourselves alone, usually because I'd been hanging out with his sister, I felt drawn to him. He had to feel it, too.

When Kase frowned, disappointed at my rejection, my heart ached.

Kase Kasun was everything I'd wanted in a guy when I was wishing for the perfect boyfriend in middle school. Back then, I was just a normal girl, my powers hadn't been triggered, and I'd attended an all-girls prep school in New York City. There was something dreamy about ending up with the All-American athletic good guy. Only, this good guy had gotten himself caught in the claws of an evil, power-hungry she-wolf before I'd arrived.

Kase's steps synced with mine, the rhythm echoing slightly in the emptying hall, and he reached in front of me to open the door leading to the parking lot. My backpack brushed against his forearm. In an effort to avoid knocking him over, I shifted the weight and nearly tipped myself over from being so top heavy. Kase used his wolf-like reflexes to catch me.

I stiffened in his arms.

"Come on, Elle," Kase whispered, and I melted. His olive skin was smooth and his dark eyes warm and inviting. Kase had been the star quarterback of our high school's football team the last two years, and there was no mistaking the muscular build under his letterman's jacket.

He brushed some of my long blond hair over my shoulder to get a better look at my face. He'd discovered all of my tells while we dated, and I could feel him analyzing me. Forcing myself to remain indifferent, I relaxed my jaw, released the inside of my cheek from between my teeth, and loosened my grip on the straps of my backpack.

"How about I take you out for coffee?" he asked. The simplicity of his invitation didn't imply anything more.

I gave him a tight smile, determined to stay strong and let him down easy. "I could use one, but you know I have training."

"Will you stay with me? Please. Even if it's only for a few minutes." Kase's voice croaked, and he gently pulled me a little closer. "We can just talk out here. I miss being with you."

My body betrayed me and leaned into him. Why couldn't we sit at Coffee Haven all afternoon and hang out with our friends? I thought after pushing Kase away for so long, it would be easier to turn him down. Last month, on Valentine's Day, I'd stayed home and claimed to be sick, all in an effort to keep Kase out of sight and out of mind.

My wall was crumbling.

"How about we get that coffee," I agreed with some hesitation, and quickly scrambled to rebuild my façade. "But as friends."

Kase slowly released me, careful to make sure I had my balance.

"I'll take what I can get." His mouth formed a tight smile, and he waved a hand in front of himself, allowing me to lead the way.

Our cars were parked side by side at the back of the lot. His blue truck made my black smart car look like a toy. He and his twin sister, Willa, shared the truck, but Willa always had archery practice after school. Her boyfriend, Tarron, also on the team, always gave her a ride home.

"Wanna ride together?" Kase asked and chuckled as he looked from his truck to the car. "I'll even try to squeeze into your car if you want to drive. Maybe you can open the sunroof so I can sit up straight."

Before I could stop myself, my hand flung out and backhanded his chest. Kase was over six feet tall, and while I was considered average height, he still towered over me. He'd always teased me about my car, and it almost felt normal to joke about it. Only, our normal had been being *together*, and we would have to figure out a new normal. My goal the past few months had been to avoid running into him altogether. Since his sister was one of my best friends, it proved more difficult than I'd anticipated.

"Haha." My fake laughter was filled with a good dose of sarcasm, and I rolled my eyes as I rummaged through the front pocket of my backpack for my keys. Kase moved around my car to open the driver's side door, and I pushed one of the buttons on my key fob as he rounded the front.

A loud honk blared, making him jump, and I couldn't contain my real laughter. The surprise on his face morphed into a genuine grin.

"That's what you get." My chest filled with warmth, even though it was freezing outside. Being with Kase made me happy, so why couldn't we ride to Coffee Haven together without it being *together?* My lips twisted as I thought, and I made my decision.

"Let's just take your truck," I said and reached for the handle of the passenger door. Kase beat me to it, and opened the door for me. Always the gentleman, he took my backpack and tossed it into the back. Pulling *A Tale of Two Cities* out of my coat pocket, I set it in the middle of the bench seat. Kase climbed into the driver seat and looked down at the novel, with its dog-eared pages and worn cover.

"Is that one for class or for fun?" he asked as he started the truck.

The novel was not what I'd call fun, but Kase was really trying. His friendship would be the one I'd miss most when I moved back to New York.

"Definitely class," I answered. "It's been too long since I've read a book for fun."

Kase put his truck into reverse and backed out of the space. He'd started to put his arm along the back of the seat when he looked behind to check for other cars, but stopped himself. He sounded easygoing, but his posture was rigid, and he almost seemed nervous. After maneuvering out of the parking lot, he relaxed a little.

"So what have you been doing for fun?" he asked softly, keeping his eyes on the road.

When I shifted to face him, the seatbelt threatened to decapitate me. Wrapping my hand around the stiff fabric, I pulled it under my arm and answered, "Mostly training and hanging out with Scarlet and your sister. My parents are still back and forth to New York on business. I almost think they feel bad about being gone so much. Last week, my dad brought a telescope home and said I needed a hobby."

"Soon you'll have track and field season to keep you busy," Kase said, and he shrugged sheepishly. "But until then, astronomy sounds cool."

"Yeah, I guess," I agreed half-heartedly.

"No, really, the sky can tell you so much, especially at night. Knowing the phases of the moon and the different constellations can help you navigate by the stars. You can even tell time by connecting Polaris to the Big Dipper."

Squinting at Kase, I wondered who the imposter was, and asked, "Who are you, and what have you done with Kase?"

He smiled and rubbed at the back of his neck with one hand. "It's me, I promise. There's a lot more that goes into patrolling the town borders than racing against Joe from one ridge to the other. And, in the state he's in, we haven't done much racing. It's not like I have to worry about the phases of the moon because I can control when I shift, but I've had to use the constellations a time or two to stay on course. And I've used the moon to help tell time. Did you know the moon has no light of its own? It's how the sun shines on it that makes it useful."

"That's cool," I said and placed a finger on my chin thoughtfully. "Maybe I'll actually tilt the telescope up and take a look."

"Tilt it up, huh?" he asked with a mischievous grin.

"You may patrol the borders, but somebody has to keep an eye out for the people in town." A giggle escaped me.

Kase slowed the truck down as we approached the four-way stop at Main and Eighth Streets. He looked over at me and asked, "And who exactly do you feel like you need to keep an eye out for?"

"Oh, no one in particular. Think of it as a neighborhood watch," I said with a smirk.

"Sounds more like stalking to me," he mumbled with a chuckle. The truck moved through the intersection, and Kase was on the lookout for a parking space.

"I don't like your tone." So I decided to flip the script. "What have you been doing for fun?"

Kase pulled into a space across the street from Coffee Haven. He kept the truck running, with the heat on, and unbuckled his seatbelt. "Hanging out with Joe mostly. He's missing Infiniti. It's kind of making him crazy. I know you're going to find this cheesy, but kind of like the moon needs the sun to be useful, I've discovered I don't have much fun without you in my life."

Shifting in my seat, I faced forward. He'd gone there. My head pressed back into the seat, and I sighed.

"I can't—no, I won't let you talk me into *this*." I waved my pointer finger between us back and forth a few times. Pausing to gauge where his mind was at, I heard nothing. Kase had blocked me. He'd learned to veil his thoughts from me by the end of our second date.

"I know you're trying to protect me—" he started.

"Don't think I'm some saint. I'm also trying to protecting me." My hand covered my heart.

"I promise to never hurt you." Kase scooted closer, and the paperback between us pressed against my thigh. He lifted his hand and cupped my jawline.

Leaning into him, I closed my eyes and whispered, "That's like promising me the moon, Kase. It kills me to see you every day in those hallways, and a few weeks ago I even stayed away, thinking it might be a little easier. But not seeing you was worse. I thought a half vampire, half dryad dating a wolf shifter was trite, but the fact that I don't know how I'm going to live in New York without you feels pathetic."

"You are anything but pathetic," Kase muttered, his warm breath caressing my cheek. "Elliot Martin, the only I question I have for you is are you doing all of this—keeping me in the friend zone, moving back to New York—for you or for your parents?"

Pulling away, I felt weak. He was the only person in town I'd ever explained my past to, and he was partially right. I wanted to press my lips against his more than anything. Even though I'd been training for over a year to build my strength, to learn to control my power, I was completely vulnerable when it came to Kase.

So I reached for the handle and opened my door. The ice-cold air flooded the cab of the truck. When Kase pulled back in shock, I turned and retreated across the street and into Coffee Haven.

CHAPTER 2

ELLE

SCOOBY GANG

Willa: Where are you E?

Elle: I'll be a few minutes late

Willa: Are you with the boy version?

Kase: I heard that, and I'm parking

Scarlet: I'm caffeinated and ready to hit the slopes

Bale: I plan to eat black diamonds for lunch

Willa: It won't officially be spring break until we're all together E! What's the hold up?

Elle: The parents are calling, give me 10

Kase: I'll order you a cinnamon latte

Bale: Awwww . . . Bro, I think you have something brown on your nose

Kase: Shut it

Elle: Uh, thanks! B4N

.   .   .

A snowboard would have been easier to fit in my smart car. Last spring break, the gang had so much fun on the slopes, we'd agreed to start the upcoming two weeks off with a friendly race. As much as Kase, Willa, Tarron, and Bale tried to convince me snowboarding was better, I wouldn't budge. Scarlet must have taken my side just to get on Bale's nerves. Skiing made me feel alive.

Skis are faster.

As I turned my car on, my cell started buzzing. Impatient as always, I figured it was my friends, so I checked it. Considering the measures my parents had gone to to protect me from texting and driving, I replied before shifting the car into drive. Then my phone started ringing. When I saw the picture of my mom and dad flash across the screen, I wondered if they had some sort of camera watching me. Pressing the green button on my steering wheel, I answered the call.

"Hey, Mom," I greeted with excitement, guessing she was calling from the airport. She and my dad had been in New York for three days and promised to be back tonight, so we could spend some of the break as a family.

"Good morning, sweetie," she said cheerily. "What are you up to today?"

"I'm going skiing with Willa and Scarlet," I said, but quickly added, "and the guys. But I'll totally be home in time to have dinner with you and Dad."

"Oh, honey, I hope it's getting easier to be around Kase." My mom sounded sympathetic, but she was over two thousand miles away. Yesterday, I'd needed her after awkwardly sipping a latte across from Kase at Coffee Haven. She'd never signed up to raise a child. Typically, a dryad was born with their tree, but I'd been abandoned at hers. I immediately felt guilty.

"It's actually gotten a lot better," I assured her, but I meant it got better when Scarlet showed up. She'd walked over from her family's herbal store to pick up a coffee for her mom. Making an excuse to leave with her, I'd told Kase I needed to buy some candles.

My mother paused, probably unsure of what to say, and I didn't hear the typical background noise I would have if she and my dad were waiting at their gate. There wasn't anything she could say to make me feel better. I just wanted her to be home, but I had a bad feeling.

"I'm glad it's better, sweetie—"

"You're not coming home, are you?" It felt like an anvil had landed on my chest.

"Well, there's a party we're expected to attend tomorrow, and your father has a meeting Monday morning," she explained. "And it won't be long until you're here with us. We're working hard to make sure things are ready for you."

"What do you mean, *ready*? I still have a month here before graduation."

My mom sighed, and I could picture her pinching the bridge of her nose. She'd done that for as long as I could remember. She and my dad filled my memories, and they assured me it was for the best. Before I'd been left in their care, a vampire killed my dryad parents. Someone from my father's clan stopped the rogue vampire before he killed me, and I have no recollection of any of it. I'd been raised balancing on a tightrope between two supernatural worlds—dryad and vampire.

"I don't know if I want that life anymore, Mom." My voice croaked. "I don't miss New York. I miss you."

"You don't mean that," my mom reasoned with an angry edge to her voice. "I mean, I miss you too, and when you get back here, you'll remember how much you love it. We have to hold up our end of the agreement with the Court in Havenwood Falls, and that includes us leaving after graduation. It will be a shock at first when you return, but maybe we can soften the blow. Your father asked me to tell you he's sending a surprise, and it should arrive later today."

My nose scrunched up in frustration. "Whatever."

I couldn't imagine what he had in mind, but maybe it included a box full of shoes. That's the only thing I could think of that could make me feel marginally better. At no point had anyone inquired about what I wanted. My father wanted to assume his duties in his family's business. My mother ached to stay close to the oak tree she was bonded with in Central Park. The Court of the Sun and the Moon had only agreed for us to stay in Havenwood Falls until I turned eighteen.

When I said goodbye, I tried to not to sound too let down, but I wasn't even sure my mom was paying attention. She'd been distracted for the duration of our conversation, even though she'd been the one to call me. Repeating the conversation in my mind over and over, I drove to Coffee Haven on autopilot. Colorado was waking from a deep winter slumber, and I could almost feel energy emanating from the earth. I was electric with anticipation, like waking up on my birthday, and even the trees seemed to stand taller, alert and ready for anything.

When I parked, I wondered how I'd arrived without driving straight through the gazebo in town square. Colorado would be in mud season soon, but the green pine trees, snowcapped mountains, and blue skies had a way of keeping one's eyes on the beauty around them instead of the mess they might trudge through. It was only last month that store owners were shoveling record-breaking amounts of snow off the sidewalks so tourists could enter their shops.

The entire Scooby Gang waited out in front of the quaint coffee shop. Willa had coined the name of our little band of nonconformists. Each of us was distinctly different, supernaturally and in appearance, but we accepted each other for who we were, and that kind of friendship was scarce in high school.

Kase jogged up to my car, the jock. He opened my door and handed me a cup of hot cinnamon goodness. "Glad you could join us," he said, with a smile that would make any girl swoon. "Want me to take your skis out of the back?"

"Please." Keeping my reply short made me feel like I had more control of my emotions. And I'd need to feel in control all week, since we'd made these plans to spend spring break together last year.

"Did I hear that right? You haven't gotten a board yet?" Bale complained in his native tongue, sarcasm. He'd been the hardest of my friends to get to know. The wall I'd built to keep Kase's and my relationship in the friend zone looked like a beaver's dam compared to the Great Wall of China he'd constructed around himself. "This would have been a great year to learn how to ski on a board. The powder this season was ridiculous. And I mean that in a good way, not in the same way I'd mean it when referring to you looking ridiculous on those skis."

"Stop giving her a hard time," Scarlet scolded, and tugged on the metal chain hanging from his belt loop and connected to his wallet. She wore her long red hair in two Dutch braids, and instead of a ski bib, she'd layered sweaters over sweaters.

Willa moved around my car to help her twin brother. They'd grown closer since she shifted last year. It also helped that Kase stopped dating her arch nemesis. It was hard to picture the cute ex-cheerleader as the leader of the Kasun Wolf Pack. But determination and loyalty ran in Willa and Kase's blood.

Tarron, Willa's boyfriend, rearranged a few of the items in the back of the Kasun twins' truck to make room for my gear. He looked up, and I could hear his thoughts as he watched Willa walk over with my skis. Tarron adored Willa, and I quickly pressed my palm to my forehead to focus.

"Are you okay?" Kase asked, and he walked over to me.

There was no danger of falling over, but I could feel his anxiety. Shaking my head clear, I answered, "I'll be fine. My parents called to tell me they aren't coming home tonight, and I think I'm just a little bummed."

"I'm sorry, Elle," he said, and slid his hand around mine. I didn't pull away. Of all my friends, he understood how much it bothered me that my parents were away so often. They'd been a couple in New York before finding me, and children hadn't been on their radar, seeing as they couldn't naturally have any of their own.

Luckily, I had wonderful friends in my life.

I glanced around us and realized something was off.

"Where's Joe?" My voice was low, trying not to draw attention to my inquiry.

Kase and Joe had always been best friends, but if Joe's lack of attendance had something to do with his search for Infiniti, I knew he wouldn't want the others to know. Kase had confided in me that Joe had a wild notion he could find his girlfriend, but Kase had been quick to shut it down.

"He's not doing great," Kase said with a frown. "All he wants to do is patrol, and I'm not sure if it's because he's looking for Infiniti or if he's trying to keep himself busy so he doesn't think about her. He's not sleeping well, and honestly, I think it'd be hard for him to see you, well, you with me."

"Me? But why?" My mouth fell open in disbelief.

Kase tugged on my hand, and as I looked up, his eyes met mine. "You didn't do anything, but he'd do anything to find Infiniti. You broke things off with me a few days after Infiniti left, and while I missed you, I got to see you almost every day. He's also been dealing with some shifter repercussions, since he recognized her as his mate. My dad tried to explain that we need to be supportive, but it was still different for him. My mom died, but Infiniti is still out there somewhere—or somewhen."

"That sounds horrible."

"It sounds like you had a pretty horrible conversation with your parents earlier."

"Thanks, but I'd rather not talk about it." Squeezing Kase's hand before letting go, I moved to help put my gear in the back of the truck. "I think I'll channel my frustration into winning this race." Glancing at Bale, I challenged, "You're going down."

He snarled at me and said, "Whether I win big or I win ugly, I'm still winning." He tucked some of his chin-length black hair behind his ear.

"You got big and ugly right," Kase said with a chuckle and nudged Bale with his elbow.

Bale shook his head and made his way around to the passenger side of the truck. "Let's just get to it, Kase," Bale said as he opened the door. "You guys are wearing me out with all your wit, and I need to save some energy for the race."

CHAPTER 3

KASE

*B*ale, Scarlet, and Elle piled into my truck. Willa would argue it was ours, but she rarely drove the old blue Chevy. Tarron and Willa opted to take Tarron's car, and I was relieved. Since Elle left me in the friend zone, Willa had been a helicopter sibling. She hovered whenever Elle was around and checked in with me constantly. Her heart was in the right place, but her nose needed to butt out.

Bale climbed into the back seat with Scarlet, surprising me. He typically called shotgun, but swore he never got carsick. I wasn't about to complain, because it meant Elle would sit next to me. Immediately, I decided to omit any conversation that would include Joe or her parents. When I looked over my shoulder, Bale gave me a knowing grin. He probably planned to make Elle as uncomfortable as possible as payback for all her trash talk.

Our drive wasn't long, but when we arrived, the slopes were busy. The next day would be the last day of ski season. Everyone grabbed their gear from the back of the truck and started suiting up. We pulled out boots, hats, gloves, boards or skis, and even a pair of snowshoes.

"I'll be the referee," Scarlet said as she stood. It looked like she'd strapped two flat canoes to her boots. Then she pulled a backpack onto her shoulders. "I brought some homework to finish."

"You won't have enough time to finish homework, babe," Bale said to her, then addressed Elle, who stood next to me. "Right, Elle? Since you'll be skiing down the mountain so fast?" He smirked.

"That's the plan," she replied and bent over to buckle her boots. As she mounted her skis, she warned, "Just stay out of my way riding that boat."

"Looks like there'll be a fleet of boats for you to have to navigate." Bale nodded to everyone else buckling into their boots and grabbing their snowboards. Then he reached for Scarlet's backpack, secured it over his shoulder, and said, "At least walk with me to the lift, babe."

"Fine." She took his hand, and they made their way.

The rest of us followed, two by two. Willa and Tarron were less affectionate, but they silently considered each other as they moved. Elle walked next to me and remained quiet. She'd keep her distance until I could break down the emotional wall she'd built. My attempts to spend time with her, without everyone else, had failed until yesterday.

Maybe Elle was having a change of heart.

Shutting her out of my thoughts was probably for the best. While I wanted her to know how much I loved her, I knew she'd believe it more if she saw my love through actions. Anyone could think they loved someone. She'd probably heard ten guys think they loved different girls in our school hallways on a daily basis.

"I wish we'd gotten some fresh powder for the race today," Elle said loud enough for everyone to hear.

"No excuses," Bale blurted over his shoulder. "But it is hard to believe we had over twenty-two feet of snow this season."

A chuckle escaped me, and Elle looked over at me with her mouth hanging open.

"I wouldn't dream of making excuses," she mocked. "But I think a wager might be in order." A dramatic pause followed as we approached the lift in silence.

Those of us riding a board had to stop and strap our front boot on, and then we glided into line. It was late enough in the morning that we'd missed the early rush, but we still had to wait a few minutes. The sun was shining, and the brisk air had already begun to freeze the tip of my nose.

"What are you thinking, Elle?" Willa wondered out loud. "Please tell me it involves the losers carrying the winner's camping gear Wednesday."

"That's a good one," Scarlet agreed, "but I'm not racing. Dang it!"

Bale laughed and wrapped an arm around her. "I'll carry your gear even if you're not racing, because Elle will be carrying mine."

"You're dreaming," Elle countered with confidence, "and you're on."

Bale nodded his acceptance of the bet and silently waved a goodbye to Scarlet as he slid up to the lift. The rest of us rode two at a time up to the mountain top. Willa and Tarron, in front of us, were enjoying each other's company as we drifted in the air. Tarron leaned in and whispered something to Willa, but Bale scanned the mountainside, probably looking for Scarlet.

Elle and I sat in awkward silence all the way up. Zoning out, I hoped to keep my mind empty, staring out over the trees. Everything Elle had done the past four months had been to keep us from hurting each other, but sitting next to my best friend, unsure of what to say, was torment. We used to be able to talk about anything.

I missed her.

"Board up," Elle warned, but her voice sounded muffled and far away. "Kase?" she asked, and the next thing I knew her arms were around me, and we were catapulted off the lift chair. "Kase!"

We slid ten feet before I realized what had happened. Instinctively, I shifted my weight to try to slow down, but my snowboard collided with one of Elle's skis. To avoid taking her down with me, I swerved into a snowbank.

"Crap! Are you okay? I'm so sorry." She glided over to me quickly, and extended her hand to help me up.

One side of her mouth pulled up in a half smile, easing my concern that she might have been injured. When she took my hand, I remembered the first time I accidentally held her hand. We were competing in the tug-of-war, and my hand slipped over hers in the middle of the game.

In that moment I knew she was special, and she'd always be special to me.

Elle let out a gasp, ripping me from the memory, and fell next to me in the snow. I looked at her and saw she'd covered her mouth, trying to hide her smile.

"What just happened?" I wasn't sure if her reaction was from losing her footing or reading my thoughts.

"I felt like making snow angels," she teased, and began to spread her limbs out as best as she could. Both her skis had come off and her poles lay haphazardly at her sides. I joined in and shoved snow in Elle's direction with one arm. She started laughing and rolled over to her stomach.

Her face was inches from mine. Everyone around us faded away, and I spoke softly, "You read my mind." My hand brushed over her knuckles, pushing aside the snow.

Could being with Elle again be as easy as this moment? Threading my fingers with hers, I took a chance. Her eyes widened, and she flinched.

"Let me help you up," I said, securing my grip.

She looked at our hands, then back at me.

"Thanks," she murmured under her breath.

"Are you two done?" Bale blurted with impatience.

Elle and I sat up to find the others waiting a few feet away. Willa wore a knowing grin, but when our eyes met, she quickly bent over to strap her back boot to her board. Everyone followed her lead.

"I was thinking we'd head somewhere a little more secluded," Tarron suggested and tilted his head to a yellow sign warning tourists away with bold black letters.

Our season passes were used as often as we could all get away from school or work or family. We each had our favorite routes, mostly black diamonds, but as supernaturals they weren't always challenging. Once in a while, we'd choose to go off the map for a more unpredictable run.

"I'm in," Bale blurted, and he jumped, pulling his knees and board into the air, and twisted to glide in the direction of the prohibited area.

"Wait up," Elle called, and scrambled to stand. She rushed to bind her boots to her skis, and used her poles to propel herself after them.

Willa held out a hand for me to take and pulled me up. Once I found my balance, we glided past the treeline together. The farther we skied off the path, the quieter it grew.

A fluttering sound behind me caught my attention. I turned to see what it could be, but there was nothing. Frozen in place, I hoped whatever I'd heard would reveal itself. As I inhaled, a familiar feeling grew in my chest. My wolf senses were on alert.

The presence hadn't felt bad or good, but mysterious. Someone or something was watching us.

"Hey," Willa said and grabbed my shoulder.

She'd startled me. I jumped, both my hands flying into a defensive pose between us.

"Willa," I growled, "I almost took a swing at you."

"Where'd you go just then?" She stepped back to give me some room.

Inspecting the area around us, I whispered, "I thought I heard—no, felt—something following us."

Willa just stood there and examined me. As wolf shifters from the same pack, we had a connection. Not only did we have a weird twin way of knowing where the other was, but Willa was one of my best friends, and she was also my alpha. If we were going to catch up with the others, I'd need to convince her everything was okay—in the forest and with Elle.

"It was probably nothing." I dismissed the feeling and waved my hand in front of me.

Willa opened her mouth and closed it. She searched the trees around us with her heightened senses. Whatever she was thinking, she wasn't saying, and that wasn't like her. Usually, she'd give me an earful on any given topic, whether I wanted to hear it or not.

"Yeah, probably nothing," she assured with her brows furrowed. Willa set her jaw and continued, "Let's go win this race."

CHAPTER 4

ELLE

I'd never felt more connected to the mountain's terrain. After I won our race, Bale wanted to double down. He figured two out of three wins would provide more sound bragging rights. His confidence didn't wane when I explained that I'd be happy to win all three races if he couldn't hear the victory in my voice. So I won them all. Bale's head hung low until I offered to make things square if he bought us all Coffee Haven. So to end the first official day of spring break, we each ordered our favorite drink and bakery item and let Bale foot the bill.

My hot mug of chai tea warmed my hands. Tarron and Scarlet also sipped on hot tea, but Willa, Bale, and Kase opted for espresso. The manager had come out from behind the counter and began to sweep under the tables. His shaggy brown hair fell over his brow while he pushed crumbs into a dustpan. Most of the tables were topped with overturned chairs, and we decided to stay until Davis kicked us out.

Davis had made a life in Havenwood Falls for his human family. He managed the coffee shop, and I frequented enough each week that I probably paid his salary. The fae owner, Willow, employed Davis, as well as supernaturals, but he didn't have a clue our magical world existed. It was safer that way.

"Hey, Davis, how are you doing?"

He looked up from his work and smiled. "Um, I'm doing pretty good, thanks for asking."

The place was typically buzzing with coffee addicts, and I realized I'd never taken the time to stop and have a conversation with the man. Sometimes I wondered if I had what it took to work as a barista. My parents would never allow it, of course. Father would have argued I didn't need the money or the temptation of fresh warm blood pulsing through customer's veins. Mother, on the other hand, would've said I was born for a greater purpose. Last year, when I'd first arrived in the little mountain town, a girl named Paisley worked behind the counter.

"Have you heard from Paisley lately?"

He looked down at the pile of debris at his feet, then back at me, and answered, "You know, she comes back to town about once a month. She'll come in for her favorite, a blueberry scone, and go on about how much she misses it here. But I know she has to be having a blast at college."

"That's great she comes back to visit." Deep down I knew that if she didn't return every month, she'd forget Havenwood Falls and everyone in it even existed. The wards that protected our town would wipe her memories, something most humans didn't know.

"Yeah," he agreed. His brows pulled together with curiosity, and he asked, "You doing okay?"

"Yeah," I said with a shrug. "I'm hanging in there. With graduation coming up, I'm just trying to figure it all out."

"Let me know if you do figure it out," he said with a laugh, and went back to work sweeping the hardwood floors. "You guys have about ten minutes before I have to lock the doors."

"Okay, thanks." Nodding, I tuned back into the enthusiastic debate Tarron and Scarlet were having about which book-to-movie adaptation was better, Harry Potter or Lord of the Rings.

"Have you seen the extended edition?" Scarlet asked, with her hands waving in the air. "I have a hard time believing you've read the novel. If you had, you'd appreciate the extra scenes and agree with me."

"Well, have you read all of the Harry Potter books?" Tarron asked, mocking her with his nose in the air.

"Yeah," Scarlet scoffed, "in third grade."

"Oh." Tarron's shoulders sunk.

Willa chuckled and took his hand. "Just tell her why you want to watch the Harry Potter movie marathon tomorrow. She'll understand, I promise."

Tarron sighed and looked from Willa to Scarlet. He closed his eyes tight and blurted, "I just finished reading the series for the first time."

He opened one eye to check for scoffing, and when he saw it was safe, he opened the other eye.

"Really?" Scarlet asked with wide eyes. "Then we have to watch Harry Potter." Her lips spread into a wide smile. "I'll even buy the makings for butterbeer!"

"I totally thought you guys were going to make fun of me," Tarron admitted.

Bale gripped the arms of his chair and said, "She may not, but I totally will."

He pushed himself up to his feet and held out a hand for Scarlet.

"Leave him alone," she warned, and handed him her empty coffee mug. "Now, let's help Davis out and take our stuff over to the counter."

After we set our dishes and mugs on the bar, Davis said, "Thanks, guys." We said our goodbyes, and as we exited, he called out, "My vote would've been for Frodo!"

Everyone laughed as we moseyed out to the parking lot behind the Main Street businesses, drawing out the inevitable. My friends were the best. When we were together, it felt like the world around us, along with the worries and responsibilities that came with it, faded away. As I grew closer to each member of our Scooby Gang, I questioned whether my feelings for Kase were real or a result of everyone coupling up.

In New York, I'd had similar feelings for someone, but they'd proven to be unreliable. Once I'd learned to trust Kase and my growing love for him, I realized it hadn't been my feelings that were uncertain. The guy I'd had feelings for was deceitful.

The girls moved toward my tiny car, and I realized my skis would make it impossible for us all to fit. I'd have to ask one of the guys to help transport us to my house. Bale's motorcycle was out of the question, and Tarron's sports car wouldn't be much help either.

"Hey, Kase, can I talk to you?" My heart skipped a beat.

My eyes met Willa's, and she took Tarron's hand and pulled him toward his car. Maybe she knew something I didn't, or maybe she was just up to no good. Willa had never once made me feel bad about breaking up with her brother, but I could tell she hadn't given up on the idea of us getting back together. Scarlet's reaction wasn't as quick, but when she realized what Willa was up to, she yanked Bale in the opposite direction from where Kase and I stood in the parking lot.

"Sure." Kase kept walking, getting off the road, and turned to face me when I stepped up on the sidewalk next to him.

The lights mounted on the old brick building and the streetlights standing at a nearby intersection made the area appear cozy, but it was frigid. I kept walking to stay warm, and he met my pace.

"Today was fun."

Kase's hands were shoved in his pockets, and suddenly I wanted him to try to hold my hand again. Not because my resolve had weakened, but because I was stronger with him at my side.

"Yeah, it was," he agreed, but he felt distant. And I'd been the one to push him away earlier when he'd asked about my parents.

Stopping short of the wooden gazebo steps, I turned to face Kase. "What are you thinking?"

Kase bit the inside of his cheek and wouldn't meet my eyes. After a few seconds of silence, he said, "Don't get me wrong. I want to tell you everything I'm thinking. But I'm curious what you're thinking?"

There was no train of thought I was following, or plan. In fact, my intention had only been to ask Kase to drive my skis to my house so the girls could ride with me. But when Kase asked me what I thought, I realized I'd been thinking too much.

So I went with my gut and slid my hand out of my pocket to reach for his. Kase's attention was drawn to the movement, and his hand hesitated. He looked up at me, and one of his eyebrows was slightly raised.

"I'm thinking, I'm sorry." My hand slid into his. "And I'm thinking I need to stop thinking so much and listen to my heart."

Kase squeezed my hand and smiled at me.

"I'm thinking it's freezing out here, and you guys can sort this all out tomorrow over butterbeer!" Willa yelled from the driver's seat of the blue Chevy. Obviously, she'd been listening with her heightened sense of hearing. "Tarron's going to give you a ride home, Kase. I'm taking the truck tonight."

The old Chevy engine roared to life, and I giggled at the sight of Willa behind the wheel. My giddiness could have also been attributed to the kiss Kase placed on the top of my hand before he walked me back to my car. Willa waited for Scarlet to jump into the truck, then pulled out onto the quiet street. With most of the shops having closed hours earlier, there weren't many people roaming around town square.

My friends wouldn't be able to get into my house without me, so I placed a quick kiss on Kase's cheek before getting into my car and leaving. Glancing in my rearview mirror, I found Kase already in Tarron's car. They turned and headed to the Kasuns' cabin, and I drove toward my neighborhood, Creekwood.

The girls' sleepover at my house had been planned as a preview to the movie marathon the following day. We'd spend the night painting nails, filling our prom Pinterest boards with potential dresses, and choreographing epic lip sync numbers. As I pulled into my driveway, I found Willa and Scarlet arguing with a man on my front porch.

"Get out of here, creep," Willa warned, waving her phone in the air, "or I'll call the sheriff." Little did the guy know, the sheriff was Willa's dad.

The man turned to see who'd pulled up, and I gasped, recognizing his profile. It couldn't be. The man standing on my porch died two years ago in New York City. My body froze in horror.

"Just hear me out," he reasoned. "You can call the cops if you want, but I arrived a couple hours ago to surprise an old friend, Elliot Martin. Do you know her? I could have sworn I had the correct address."

He looked down at his phone, and the light from the screen illuminated his face. It wasn't the man I'd feared after all, but his not-so-little brother. Marcel Cushing looked different, older, but that was impossible. Being a vampire, he hadn't grown up physically like me. I'd been a dryad before being bitten, but my parents discovered my dryad blood was stronger than the vampire who'd tried to sire me. Still, Marcel bore an uncanny resemblance to his older, sired brother. The only reason they called each other brother was because they'd been bitten by the same vampire and raised to control their urges by him. Marcel's dark hair was shaggy, but perfectly mussed to appear casual, though the Cushings were the most formal family I'd ever encountered. Marcel had deep-set brown eyes, and his fair skin could be attributed to his lack of exposure to the sun.

"Elle, do you know this guy?" Scarlet asked from behind Willa. She looked over Willa's shoulder at me and frowned.

Slowly walking around my car, I knew in the back of my mind that he couldn't hurt me, but I was still cautious. My mind thought through a couple different ways to convince Willa and Scarlet to move away from him, but Willa had probably already deduced what Marcel was, a vampire. The Cushings were one of the oldest vampire families in New York, and I understood firsthand how much power he wielded.

"Yeah, I know him." With each step closer, I attempted to read his thoughts. "But I don't know why or how he's here."

The reason my family moved to Havenwood Falls was for the protection it offered from the outside world, from my past. If Marcel wasn't supposed to be in town, there's no way he would've been able to drive past the town border, let alone up to my house and wait on the front porch, without a slew of supernaturals being magically alerted.

"Your parents flew me out," Marcel said as he stepped down from the porch toward me.

Willa let a low growl rumble in her chest.

Marcel glanced back at her with wide eyes, then he explained, "Since the Martins' return was delayed, they thought it would be a good idea for me to visit. Special permission from the Court and everything. Think of it as reintroducing Elle's old life in bite-sized pieces." He sounded kind and charming.

Whether he meant to be punny or not, his wording wasn't lost on Willa. She smiled in response with a menacing, overly toothy grin. What she didn't know was Marcel had always been bad at telling jokes. While his older brother had been suave and charismatic, Marcel hadn't cared about the bloodlines and politics. He'd been called unrefined and annoying in the socialite company our families kept.

"I'm not sure my parents thought this through." My eyes rolled, remembering the earlier conversation with my mother. "You must be the surprise package she mentioned this morning."

"Too bad you can't stamp him *return to sender* and let him be on his way," Scarlet clipped curtly, and propped a hand on her hip.

My fingers pinched the bridge of my nose, trying to come up with a way to deal with Marcel and our current predicament. My parents couldn't have expected him to stay in our home. Marcel had been my friend growing up, but after what happened to his brother, I'd expected him to blame me and never want to see me again.

"I need some time to process, Marcel." Trying to hide the unease in my voice, I explained, "It's only, we have this sleepover planned, and a movie marathon, and camping—"

Saying it out loud helped me stay grounded. Marcel wasn't a part of my plans or my life in Havenwood Falls, and I didn't know if I wanted him to have any part in my life. But I couldn't be rude.

"What she's trying to say is, we'll call you tomorrow," Willa cut in and walked over to stand next to me. "Do you have a place to stay tonight? I can call my dad to help set you up at the inn, or somewhere more secluded without windows."

Scarlet giggled at Willa's humor, and I felt the corners of my mouth pull up a little. He *was* a vampire. He didn't need a daylight ring, but bloodlust was an issue for most vampires so young. The only reason I could control my appetite was because of my hybrid blood.

"The Court of your quaint town has already made arrangements for me, but thank you," Marcel said with a tight smile. "I can understand your surprise at seeing me after two years, but before I go, I need you to understand that I've come to apologize. I'm sorry it took so long to find out where your parents brought you. I'm sorry I didn't fight for our friendship. What happened to Armand was tragic—" He sounded heartbroken.

"I don't want to talk about him." My words cut him off, and I squeezed my hands into fists, nearly breaking the skin of my palms with my fingernails. "Please."

Willa and Scarlet had never pressed for details about why my family moved to Havenwood Falls, and I didn't want them finding out from a stranger.

Willa stepped in front of me protectively. "It's getting late." Her nostrils flared, and her lips tightened.

"Tomorrow, then." Marcel nodded reluctantly and walked straight to a silver sedan with a familiar car rental logo stuck to the bumper. Before he ducked his tall lean frame into the driver's seat, he glanced at us. His eyes were wet.

None of us moved a muscle until his red taillights disappeared beyond the Creekwood Country Club sign. Scarlet made for the truck first and started unloading. Her determination to only make the trip once broke our silence and probably woke the neighbors. A pair of snowshoes clattered to the ground when Scarlet tripped over herself trying to beat Willa to the front door.

"So what's on the schedule?" Scarlet asked, and she dropped all of her possessions in the middle of the living room floor.

My teeth bit at the inside of my lip, worrying about what Scarlet and Willa would think of me when they found out why I really ended up in Havenwood Falls. Would they want to leave when they found out I was involved in a murder? Could they understand I had no other choice if I'd wanted to survive Armand's attack?

"I think we'll tell ghost stories first." My body collapsed onto the couch. "I have a really good one." My voice lowered and sounded grim.

My friends joined me, and I started to tell a story about a girl who wanted to be loved. She'd thought she'd found the love she desired, but it was only a manipulation to gain access to her hybrid blood.

"In a moment of weakness, I'd agreed to allow Armand a taste. My sweet dryad blood proved too tempting, and Armand got carried away. I begged him to stop, and pushed him away, but he continued to pursue me. Marcel overheard our scuffle and came to my rescue, only Armand didn't see it that way. My blood had made him crazy. When Marcel entered my room, Armand thought his younger brother was trying to steal me for himself."

"What happened next?" Willa asked, sounding worried, and leaned forward.

"Armand lunged for Marcel, and the two wrestled across the floor, breaking my antique wooden rolltop desk. The legs had been snapped in half, and Marcel grabbed one of the splintered ends in defense. So when Armand charged Marcel again, the makeshift stake pierced his heart."

"Oh, man, Elle," Willa soothed and laid a hand on my knee. "I'm so sorry you were attacked, and had to witness what happened between Armand and Marcel."

"Me too." It had been horrible. "Until tonight, my parents and Kase were the only people I ever told." Sharing with my friends had only made me feel freer.

Fear hadn't kept me from telling Willa and Scarlet, but it was the darkest part of my past. Kase hadn't been any different, and because of his support, he deserved to know about Marcel's visit.

"Do you guys mind if I make a call?"

Willa and Scarlet nodded their consent. Reaching for my cell, I pulled it out of my back pocket and pressed my finger to the screen.

CHAPTER 5

KASE

*I*t had taken everything in me not to shift and guard Elle's house that night. She assured me Marcel didn't mean any harm. The memories were hard for her, but Elle was strong. And when she needed a distraction, I knew Willa and Scarlet would be there for her.

"Hey, man," Tarron said, and nudged me with his elbow. "You okay?"

"Yeah." My eyes felt dry, and I blinked a few times to wet them.

Tarron's classic car was more comfortable than Elle's smart car, but not much bigger. Driving through the heart of Havenwood Falls, I'd been in a daze. We passed the high school, and the next right would usher us to Creekwood Estates. The neighborhood had been built over a couple decades and the homes were at least twice the size of our family's cabin in the woods.

"I know we're headed to Elle's to talk about this guy, Marcel," Tarron started as we turned, "but I'm curious what your take is?"

Shrugging, I said, half serious, "I want to hurt him."

Tarron chuckled, and when I didn't laugh he glanced at me and grimaced. "Okay."

"Honestly, I don't know. He's an old friend of Elle's, and he saved her life back when she lived in New York. There's more to the story, but it's not mine to tell."

"I get that, but from what Willa texted last night, it's not a happy reunion," Tarron revealed, encouraging me.

"I'm not sure Elle even knows how to process Marcel showing up. He arrived without any warning, and I think Elle wants our help to find out if he's really in town for the reasons he explained last night." I said, trying to sound neutral.

The last thing Elle needed was for us to speculate crazy conspiracies about why Marcel was visiting. I'd come up with at least three ideas since we'd turned onto Blackstone Road. As we pulled into Elle's driveway, I compartmentalized my cynicism. If Elle read my mind and I hinted at thoughts of Marcel sweeping her off her feet or him making grand gestures, she'd think I was jealous and immature.

I might have been both, but she didn't need to know it.

As we approached the front door, I noticed the T-shirt Tarron wore under his coat. It read, *I solemnly swear I'm up to no good.* He'd really been looking forward to the movie marathon.

I'd really been looking forward to holding Elle's hand during said movies. Last night, I thought we were finally back on the same path. Baby steps. The last thing I wanted to do was scare Elle off, and I didn't mind taking my time. If I had my way, we'd have the rest of our lives together.

Holding my hand out in front of Tarron, I asked, "Can I tell you something?"

"Sure, anything," he replied, and with concern, he crossed his arms over his chest and met my eyes.

"The problem is, you can't tell Willa." My eyebrow raised skeptically.

Tarron pressed his lips together in a straight line and fell silent.

"If it makes a difference, she wouldn't even know to ask you about it."

He raised his chin slightly and consented. "If that's the case, shoot."

My words rushed out uncontrollably. "I applied to NYU just before the holidays, and I'm waiting for an email to find out if I got in.

What if I don't get in? Then Elle will leave in June, and I'll be stuck here. Or, what if I do get in? My—"

"Your sister will freak, and I'll be stuck here with her. You can never tell her I knew about this," he begged, sounding anxious.

"I won't tell her." Avoiding eye contact, I looked down at my feet and said bleakly, "I may not have to say anything at all if I'm not accepted."

"One thing at a time, my man," Tarron encouraged me, and patted my arm. "Let's figure out this Marcel character, then we can tackle the possibility of you moving several states away."

My lips spread into a grin. "Maybe *tackle* isn't the best word to use. Knowing Willa, she may decide to tackle me when she finds out."

Tarron nodded and asked, "We good?"

"Yeah."

He lifted a fist to the wooden door, and knocked three times. From inside, we heard the three girls holler to come in. The door was unlocked, and as it swung open, the scent of bacon and cinnamon filled my nostrils. Someone was cooking breakfast.

Anytime I'd been invited to the Martins' house for dinner, I felt the need to wear a suit. The modern art, sleek furniture, and minimal approach to decorating made the place feel less like a home and more like a museum.

"We're back here," Elle called from the kitchen.

Elle's house in New York probably looked similar, and I wondered if her father did the decorating. Mr. Martin had the suave charm and riches of a character like Jay Gatsby, as well as the mystery. The difference was Mr. Martin could live forever.

"Did you guys get any sleep last night?" Tarron asked as we walked into the open living area.

Willa sat on a stool at the island that separated the space into three parts—living, dining, and kitchen. She looked up with puffy pink eyes and said, "Sleep? Who can sleep with unpainted nails?"

She wiggled her violet fingernails in the air at us.

"So what you're saying is you'll need a nap later?" Tarron asked and looked over at the entertainment system longingly.

A flat screen as wide as the wall was mounted at one end of the room in front of a large sectional, brushed silver appliances nestled between white cabinets at the opposite end, and the back wall was made up of windows.

"I promise to stay awake through *Goblet*. Just don't hate me if I rest my eyes during *Order*," Willa pleaded, then she glanced at Elle, who looked annoyed. "That is, if we have time to watch all the movies. You do realize we'll be up all night watching them."

"If we have time?" Tarron whined. "I got up before nine during spring break for this. And I'll stay up as long as it takes."

"I know, but Elle needs our help." Willa tried to console both her boyfriend and her best friend. Her patience had not only put out a few fires between our friends, but it was preparing her for becoming alpha of our pack.

Elle used tongs to carefully turn a piece of bacon. Scarlet opened the oven door, and the fresh smell of warm bread and cinnamon filled the space. She moved the hot baked goods to the island and started icing them.

"Where's Bale?"

Scarlet's eyes darted from Tarron to Willa, then to me, before she answered with a frown, "Sleeping in."

"Is there anything I can help with?" To be nice, I'd asked in the general direction of the kitchen. Cooking hadn't ever been a talent of mine, but I could hold my own. It was another thing for Willa not to help. She'd never been good at cooking anything that didn't involve a microwave.

"No, I'm almost done," Scarlet answered.

Elle looked at me, then down at her frying pan. With a grin she said, "I don't trust you with the bacon."

"Fair enough." With a smile, I asked, "You mind if I go outside until it's ready?"

"Not at all," Elle said casually.

My favorite part of the Martins' property was their backyard. Elle's mom was a dryad, and even though the tree she was bonded to stood in Central Park, she made their yard feel like home. The patio was lined with potted plants, and a few spruce and pine trees provided privacy. A pair of oak trees were located at the center of the space, and a hammock hung between them.

A shot of cold air hit me as I slid the back door open. Quickly closing it, I glanced through the glass behind me. The thought of us all disbanding after graduation made my chest feel tight. Walking to the hammock, I wondered if any of us would leave Havenwood Falls and forget. The town had wards protecting it, but there were also magical precautions taken so that anyone who left without returning for more than a few weeks would lose every memory of the place and its inhabitants.

With less coordination than I'd hoped, I leaned back into the green hammock. It rocked back and forth, and the sunlight above appeared to be moving as it shone through the bare branches. The same sun would shine in New York if I was accepted to NYU, but returning to Havenwood Falls before the end of every moon cycle would be crucial to my plan working.

Elle didn't want to leave, and I could feel it. Her sense of loyalty and obligation to her parents wouldn't allow her to stay.

And I didn't want her to leave, so I'd study law at NYU and come back to Havenwood Falls in order to stay connected with my family. My gut told me her parents weren't telling her everything, or maybe they didn't know everything. Like other hybrids in town, the mixed bloodlines had a way of changing supernatural rules and traditions. Celeste Long came to mind. She'd only just learned she's part fae, and to go through it all without her mom to guide her had to be difficult and scary.

"Hey," Elle called from the deck, "breakfast is ready!"

Behind me, I heard the door slide shut and carefully sat up. As my weight shifted, the hammock swung, and I jumped with super agility to my feet. Being a shifter had perks.

"Nice move," Elle said with a giggle. "If only you'd been that quick on your feet the last time we were back here."

She meant when we lay back here enjoying the last day of summer. When we both attempted to stand at the same time, we'd both ended up on our butts in the grass. It would have been a dream come true if we could've stayed like that, laughing without a care in the world.

"Being a klutz is part of my charm," I said with a smile. "But it only seems to happen when I'm around you."

"I wanted to let you know, without everyone else listening in—" Elle started.

"And by everyone you mean my sister," I interrupted, amused.

"Yeah," she said with a raised eyebrow. "Well, I wanted to tell you that last night was—"

"Not a mistake." Interrupting her, I was not amused, but more worried about where she was going with this conversation. "Following your heart—"

"Kase, stop interrupting me," Elle said through gritted teeth. "It's annoying, and not what I was going to say."

"I'm sorry." Looking down at my brown boots, I waited for the inevitable.

Elle placed a hand on my chest, and my heart pounded underneath it. The scent of balsam with notes of berries grew stronger the closer she stood. Elle didn't smell like fake, sugary, mass-produced lotions; her scent was one of a kind.

"You don't need to apologize. I've given you plenty of reasons to react that way. I'm the one who's sorry, and last night was a step back in the right direction. Marcel being here doesn't change the way I feel about you. That's what I was trying to say." Her words had been spoken earnestly.

Elle's hand lingered on my chest, and I was tempted to lean forward and kiss her full lips. Behind her, I heard the back door slide open. Our friends had the worst timing. Glaring over Elle's head, I found Bale gnawing on a slice of bacon.

"Dude, I'm not promising there will be anything left once I head in for seconds," he warned with a lopsided grin.

"I'm so glad you could join us," I said sarcastically, and took Elle's hand in mine. We walked toward the deck. "But if you eat more than your share of the bacon, I'll have Tate and Conall make your life miserable."

"Whatever," Bale said, unimpressed, waving his bacon in the air.

But I understood how Bale dealt with threats that hit too close to home. My reactions were similar. The dragon shifter knew I couldn't take him in a supernatural fight, but I could convince my two oldest brothers to torture him. And if it that didn't carry enough weight, I always had our dad to use as a last resort. No one wanted to be on Sheriff Ric Kasun's bad side.

Elle and I entered the kitchen, and I watched as Bale bypassed the food and plopped onto the couch next to Scarlet. Everyone else had made a plate and found a spot to eat. Elle topped her plate with a reasonable three strips of bacon and cinnamon roll. I, on the other hand, piled three cinnamon rolls and a handful of bacon onto mine. A glass of milk and a mug hot tea sat at the end of the island.

Elle nodded for me to take the milk after she'd picked up her mug. Following her to the sectional, I made myself comfortable beside her. My stomach rumbled, and I couldn't wait to dig in.

"I'll get the movie started," Tarron said with excitement as he reached for the remote. The large screen lit up on the wall, and Tarron clicked through to sign into an app. "I bought digital copies yesterday."

Elle sat her plate down on the coffee table in front of us, cleared her throat, and said, "Do you guys mind if we discuss my friend, Marcel, before it starts? I was hoping we could go to the inn around lunchtime so I can introduce everyone."

"I'd be happy to meet him." My voice sounded a little too eager. The truth was I'd be happier to see him leave.

Bale chuckled, and asked, "Is he staying? I was under the impression we were meeting him so we could run him out of town."

"I'm not sure how I want to handle Marcel being here," Elle said with furrowed brows. "If he's in Havenwood Falls to apologize, I feel like I should give him a chance."

"Why else would he be here?" Willa asked.

"I'm not sure. I just have a weird feeling about it," Elle admitted hesitantly.

"You know, we should attempt the whole *keep your enemies closer* thing," Tarron suggested, his eyes still glued to the television. "If only we had an invisibility cloak."

"How would an invisibility cloak help?" Willa tilted her head in confusion.

"Oh, I just want one," Tarron admitted nonchalantly. "Since Marcel's a vampire, it would take some serious magic to get the truth out of him. And while we have the resources here in town, there's no way the Court would approve it."

"Tarron's right. If the Court gave him permission to be here, it would take incriminating evidence to convince them to help us," I agreed.

"Then we keep him close," Elle said with a hint of inflection in her voice, making it sound more like a question. "I don't want to jump to any conclusions, but better safe than sorry."

"He may be here to see you, but to be safe, we won't leave you alone with him for a moment," Scarlet offered, and laid a hand on Elle's knee supportively.

"Thanks," Elle said and gave her a tight smile. "But I'm sure this whole visit will turn out harmless."

"Well, if that's settled, let's get started," Tarron said, and waved the remote in the air. "Revelio!"

CHAPTER 6

KASE

e'd only tackled two of the movies, but promised Tarron we'd finish the rest after lunch in town. Piling into my truck, the six of us drove to the town square. Bale, Scarlet, and Tarron sat in the backseat, and Willa and Elle shared the front seat with me. Searching for a parking space, I spotted one near the police station. With it being spring break and lunchtime, the area was busy.

"I hate when we have to park this far," Bale complained as he stepped out of the truck. We'd have to walk across the town square to reach Whisper Falls Inn.

Willa glanced at me, as if asking permission to explain to him, and I shrugged my consent. It was a twin thing. Most of the time we followed each other's thought process, but over the years, puberty had mangled a few of our attempts at working our dad over. As wolves, our pack could communicate telepathically, but in our human form we went with our guts.

"Bale, it's crowded downtown," Willa began, "and we're here to find out Marcel's motives. If for some reason our new friend reacts badly, we'll want some backup." She nodded at the police station.

"What do you think he's going to do? Attack us? Go on a bloodsucking rampage in broad daylight?" Bale scoffed.

"Of course not," Willa said, agitated.

"Chill. Have you considered what this conversation will lead to if we really want to know what this guy's up to?" I said, knowing we'd have to act like we wanted him around, and coax him into revealing the truth.

Bale pressed his lips together in a flat line and shook his head.

I added, "Let's just say, we can't come right out and ask him why he's here, and I hope Marcel likes butterbeer." My hand took Elle's as we walked.

She laced her fingers between mine, and said, "Oh, we don't need—"

"No, he's right," Tarron interjected. "We've got to get to the bottom of this. Did you talk to your parents again?"

"No, my dad's in some meeting, and my mom is convening with the other dryads in Central Park," Elle answered with a hint of agitation.

"Maybe they don't even know he's here. He definitely gave me a Malfoy vibe last night," Scarlet added, and wrapped her sweater tighter around herself.

"I bet he's a Slytherin," Tarron said with a mischievous grin.

"As much as I dislike this idea, the point I was trying to make is that we'll need to invite Marcel to spend time with us this week." I knew if I tried to hide how I felt, Elle would probably be able to read my mind anyway. "If there's something up with Marcel, he'll probably want to avoid being anywhere near the police station or City Hall. So we'll invite him to ride back to Elle's with us."

"Um, that won't work," Bale said with a hint of arrogance. "Your cab is already full with all of us in it."

"It is," Willa chimed in. "I guess I'll have to drag all of you into the station to borrow the keys to Dad's truck."

"Nice," Tarron said with a nod. "If anyone can scare the truth out of Marcel, it would be Sheriff Kasun, especially when he's carrying his gun."

We all laughed, and I almost felt bad for Tarron when I looked over at him and realized he hadn't meant it as a joke. Beyond him, in the distance, I saw Brice Blackstone, with his brown floppy hair, skate by, probably headed to his family's wine-tasting storefront, Soothing

Sips. The guy was a year younger than us, but we'd grown up with the same familial obligations. In addition to my dad being sheriff, my family's outdoor supply store, Backwoods Sport & Ski, was located across the street.

Inspecting the block across from us, I started with the display of skis on the sidewalk in front of Backwoods. A few other faces were familiar, and I was surprised to see Joe exiting Howe's Herbal Shoppe, a stranger following him. Joe looked up and recognized us, but darted off in the opposite direction.

The stranger behind him wore a nice black pea coat and carried at least four shopping bags. Initially, I figured he was a tourist visiting for spring break. Then he glanced up, and I felt him recognize Elle.

Elle stiffened beside me.

"He's just walked out of the Howe's shop," I grumbled, and glanced at Scarlet.

She conducted her own inspection of the situation, and blurted, "Why on earth would he want a scented candle or souvenir mug?"

"Do you think you could ask your mom what he bought?" He didn't look like the type of guy who collected souvenir coffee mugs.

"Sure," Scarlet answered, "but how will you guys keep him occupied?"

"Are you sure we have to invite him to join us?" Elle bit her bottom lip, then suggested, "What if we just have coffee with him?"

Willa tucked a piece of hair behind her ear and said, "We need to tell him about our plans this week, and see if he wants to tag along."

"This week? I thought we might invite him over today, but I don't want him intruding on our camping trip," Elle complained disapprovingly.

The group had changed course, and we walked to meet Marcel in front of the herbal shop. Marcel didn't exactly blend in with the natives. Most of the town's male inhabitants wore jeans, layers of flannel, and scuffed boots. Marcel waited patiently until we stepped up to greet him. Elle shared everyone else's names, and when she introduced me, Marcel's eyes widened in surprise.

"Kase, it's nice to meet you." Marcel offered his hand to shake, and I realized I'd have to release Elle's hand to shake his.

"The pleasure is all mine." My hand gripped his and gave a sturdy shake.

As my hand fell back to my side, Elle quickly took hold of it and made a point of stepping closer to me. The gesture didn't go unnoticed by Marcel. He shifted his weight from one foot to the other.

"Nice boots," Willa said and pointed at his feet.

Marcel's brows furrowed, then he looked down and said, "Thanks, I just bought them. That store, Backwoods, sells everything, even sweatshirts that say *Take a hike, because people suck!*" He sounded amused.

Bale laughed and said, "That's one of my favorites. I'm not sure where Tate gets all of his quips, but I resemble most of them."

"Don't you mean relate to?" Marcel asked, confused.

Bale shoved his hands in his pockets and answered, "Nope."

"Well," Scarlet interrupted, "I'm going to run in and say hi to my mom real quick. I'll be right back."

She stepped toward Howe's Herbal Shoppe, where a tourist could find the perfect Havenwood Falls postcard or essential oils, and a local supernatural could purchase a magical talisman or potion. Marcel watched as Scarlet walked into her family's store, and a set of bells hanging inside rang. A cloud of herbal scents filled the air around us. Then Marcel turned back to the rest of us, composed. He pulled his bags up and started buttoning his coat.

"Can I hold something for you?" Elle asked.

"I think I've got it all," Marcel assured. "So, have you guys eaten lunch?"

"Not yet," Willa answered. "Do you want to go with us to Burger Bar?"

"Sure, if it means I get to hang out with Elle, I'm in." Marcel smiled at Elle, but his smile faltered as he took each of us in.

His enthusiasm came across as fake to me, but Elle smiled back at him like she didn't catch his excessively flattering tone. Her hand still secure in mine, I squeezed it softly. She looked up at me and gave me a quick wink. Could she read his mind?

"You can ride with us," Willa offered, and pointed over her shoulder toward the police station. "We're just parked over there."

"Actually, I should probably go put this stuff back in my room at the inn." Marcel shrugged, lifting the bags hanging from his arms.

The sound of bells chimed, and Scarlet joined us on the sidewalk, smelling of cloves and orange. Her lips were twisted as tightly as her braided red hair. She rocked onto her toes and back to her heels, and finally asked, "So what's the plan?"

"Burgers," Bale informed, "but Marcel here says he needs to take his souvenirs back to his room first."

"Cool," Scarlet said with a smile. "You probably saw Burger Bar on your way into town. You can meet us there."

"But," Willa started with a frown, "we could all ride together. It would be fun."

She attempted to sound casual, but was as successful as Marcel at blending in. Willa wanted to see her plan play out, but I could tell Scarlet was up to something too. It made sense to keep Marcel close and find out how he'd react to authority. My dad wasn't an official member of the Court of the Sun and the Moon, but until Willa was ready to take over as alpha of the Kasun pack, our dad served in the role. He would have been made aware of any and all supernatural visitors.

"I appreciate the offer, Willa," Marcel said with a tight smile. "But I don't want to be a burden, and don't say I wouldn't be. I'll just meet you guys at Burger Bar."

"If you insist," Scarlet approved. "We'll go get a table and order some shakes. What kind is your favorite?"

"Uh, vanilla," Marcel answered, looking perplexed with furrowed brows. "So I'll meet you there as soon as I put these away."

"Perfect." Elle beamed. "Then we'll head that way."

Elle squeezed my hand and tugged me to turn around and follow her. The group of us made our way back across the square, and as we passed the fountain at its center, I glanced back to find Marcel watching us. He hadn't moved. At the end of the block behind him, Joe stood, observing the scene with a blank face. Weird.

"Vanilla?" Scarlet marveled.

"I can't believe you're surprised," scoffed Willa.

"I can't believe you two are still talking about milkshakes." Tarron grimaced, trying to hide his disappointment from Willa by turning to Scarlet. "What did he buy from your mom?"

"Well, I have good news and bad news. My mom wasn't in the shop. My grandmother said she had a few errands to run before lunch," Scarlet informed, then paused.

We'd reached the truck, and all piled inside. I started the engine once everyone had buckled in, and pulled into the flow of traffic. In the distance, Marcel was walking into the inn. With a hint of impatience, I asked, "Was that the good news or the bad news?"

"Neither, I was trying to decide which to tell you first," she answered.

"The good," Elle requested. "Give us the good news first."

"Okay, my grandmother remembered selling some valerian. It's an herb that helps people rest," Scarlet explained.

"That makes sense." Elle sounded relieved. "Vampires don't really sleep regularly. You know, they tend to rest during the day. So if Marcel is trying to fit in, he'd need to take the valerian to help him shift to our sleep cycle."

"Yeah, but it might have been Joe who bought the Valerian. He's been having a hard time sleeping the last few months." My intel didn't help. Everyone sat in silence for a few seconds before I asked, "What's the bad news?"

"He also bought something from our back room," Scarlet said with wide eyes. "Something to give the herbs a supernatural kick—"

"Still makes sense," Elle interrupted. "Valerian on its own wouldn't do the trick for a vampire."

"Or a troubled shifter," I added.

"But you guys know my grandmother can get a little spacey sometimes. My mom and I think she picks and chooses who she's coherent with, but there's no way to really tell," Scarlet worried.

We all waited for Scarlet to continue, because we understood her worry wasn't limited to this one instance. Ruby Howe was a legend in the supernatural community, but as she aged, her mind wandered more and more. From a human's perspective, she came across as extremely quirky and forgetful. Scarlet and her mother, Rose, had to keep tabs on Ruby constantly to make sure she didn't accidentally misuse her powers.

"She said something about a disillusioned, charming man coming by, so I went to check the books. Gram is supposed to write everything down, but when I looked at the latest entry, it had been jumbled," Scarlet said as she rubbed her temples.

"Jumbled?" asked Bale, confused.

Looking at him in my rearview mirror, I could see he was focused on Scarlet. He reached his hand over and placed it on her knee consolingly. We waited for her to answer, while the sound of the truck's heater let out a low whistle. As we approached Burger Bar, it was funny to see the high school's parking lot deserted, and the best burger joint in town buzzing.

"It looked like Gram tried to write something down in the ledger, but she must have been confused because she wrote one of her mysterious incantations. Her chicken scratch is already hard to read, but when it's a jumbled mix of rhyming words, it's impossible to make sense of." Scarlet shook her head and added, "It was gibberish. All I could make out was, *seener unseen, fader evade.*"

After I parked, everyone exited the truck, and I repeated the words in my head. Tarron headed inside to get us a table, Bale pulled Scarlet in his arms and whispered to her, and Willa gave me the *eye*. It was never good when she made that face at me. All of her features appeared to shrink, but her right eye seemed to double in size. There was no way I would be able to talk to her alone. It was like every car that parked at the school on a daily basis had decided to park at Burger Bar.

"Hey," Elle said, smiling as she walked around the front of the truck to me. "I need to run to the ladies' room. Willa," she called back over her shoulder, "wanna come with?"

It wasn't a good idea to wonder why girls always traveled to the bathroom together, but the thought escaped its compartment. Elle turned back to face me and playfully shoved my shoulder. Stepping back, I held my hands up in surrender.

"It's one of the greatest mysteries of all time."

"What are you two talking about?" Willa asked.

"Oh, nothing," Elle answered. "I'll be right back. Unless you want to go with?"

"Nah, I'm good for now," Willa said and waved her away. "I'll stay with the boy version and make sure he doesn't get into any trouble."

Elle giggled and weaved between the cars parked in the drive-in stalls. I inspected the area, wanting to make sure we could speak freely. Willa hooked her arm around mine and pulled me with her.

"I have a really bad feeling about Marcel," she cautioned with a frown.

"I do too, but it's mainly because I think he came here to win Elle over," I admitted. "I can't think it around her, but her parents were glad to see us break up, and I wouldn't be surprised if her father already married her off to some vampire family to solidify his position on their council."

The life she'd lived in New York hadn't all been miserable, but the way her father's vampire clan orchestrated bloodlines and revered supernatural species was creepy. At first when she'd described it, I thought her life in the city had been filled with formal galas, private school, and French tutors. Underneath, the clans weren't all bad, but some valued power more than anything else.

"That's horrible to think, and I can't imagine Mr. Martin doing that," Willa scolded, and she was right. Elle's dad may not have liked the idea of me in her life, but he wouldn't force her to marry someone. "But Marcel strikes me as someone who cares more about how he's perceived than who he really is. He's fake, and I'm not sure we'll get the truth out of him."

"You may be right, but we have to try."

And, as if he'd heard us saying his name, Marcel Cushing turned into the Burger Bar parking lot and waved at the two of us, sporting a wide, duplicitous smile.

CHAPTER 7

ELLE

*B*efore I left the bathroom, I closed my eyes and took a few deep breaths. Controlling my mind and the thoughts I allowed in was more difficult with Marcel around. Because of my desire to want to know why he was in town, my guard hadn't been up. As vampires, we couldn't read each other's minds unless we fed from each other. So it didn't make sense for my mind to reach out to his; it was merely habit.

Walking over to the table Tarron had saved, I recognized a few classmates enjoying spring break too. Joseph Greg, Kase's best friend, stepped away from the diner's counter with a paper bag. He glanced in my direction and frowned. Joe's blond hair fell over his brow, longer than normal, unkempt. A pallid complexion and sunken features made me question whether he was really eating the food he carried or just keeping up appearances.

"Joe," I called out as he reached the exit, but he either didn't hear me over the crowd of enthusiastic teens or ignored me. When we'd noticed Joe leaving the Howes' store before Marcel, I'd thought I picked up some anxiety from Kase. At the time, I figured it was from meeting Marcel, but it made more sense for Kase to be anxious about Joe and how he looked.

My eyes surveyed Burger Bar's dining room. The three walls of windows revealed cars parked in every drive-in stall, and the booths and tables weren't any different. The place was crawling with teenagers. I avoided looking too long at one booth in particular, because Ana Novak sat with her bestie, Marie, and a few of the Kasun pack guys from the football team. The group laughed hysterically at one of the boys suffering from brain freeze after chugging his milkshake.

Bale and Scarlet were sitting with Tarron, and four empty chairs were tucked under the table. The scent of fresh fried food pulled me to the basket in front of Tarron like a waft of air in a cartoon. I sat in one of the red-and-white-cushioned chairs across from him and found a few tater tots left at the bottom. When I reached for one, Tarron flinched.

"What? I can't have one?"

"Sure, but they were here when I sat down." He shrugged and tilted the basket toward me. Looking at Bale, who sat next to him, he warned, "I'm sure you don't care."

Bale shunned the greasy goodness, lifted his chin in the air, and folded his arms over his chest.

Maggie Hopkins, one of the owners, skated by and circled the table. "What can I get started for you guys?"

She pulled out a pad of paper from her apron and reached for a pencil tucked behind her ear. She took each of our orders. Bale and Scarlet recited their usuals, and Tarron ordered for himself and Willa. Kase's order was easy, and I guessed for Marcel. Then I ordered my favorite—the steak finger basket with tots instead of fries and a chocolate shake. Maggie grabbed the red basket of old tots before she skated away and clipped our ticket to a wheel hanging between the soda bar and the kitchen.

The front door squeaked as it opened, and roller skates clattered on the black and white checkered linoleum repeatedly. It wasn't until we heard a collision—specifically a tray toppling to the floor—that we all turned to find Marcel covered in milkshake and french fries. Kase and Willa stood behind him untouched, and one of the carhops looked mortified by the accident.

"I'm so sorry," she said, and began wiping the front of Marcel's coat.

Everyone in the diner clapped like we were back in elementary school. Marcel's jaw clenched, and his body stiffened. Willa wedged herself between Marcel and the carhop and encouraged her to stop.

"How about you go get a mop," she suggested, "and I'll help with this." Willa held her hand out in front of Marcel and waved it in a circular motion.

The carhop skated away, making room for Willa, Marcel, and Kase to move around the mess. Marcel worked on unfastening the buttons on his coat and hung it over the back of a chair at the end of the table. Kase made his way to sit next to me, and Willa took the seat next to Tarron.

After a few moments of awkward silence, Tarron blurted, "So, Marcel, have you read the Harry Potter books?"

∼

Lunch was delicious as usual. Whenever an awkward topic came up, someone just shoved a burger in their mouth, or in my case, a steak finger. Marcel went from complimenting Tarron's taste in literature to agreeing with Bale about snowboards being faster than skis.

When the topic shifted to life after high school, Bale became quiet. Out of all of us, he was having the hardest time with the idea of all of us growing up. Scarlet would have talked about his aversion to adulting, but I wasn't sure she even knew what bothered him so much about graduating and going to college.

We all leaned back in our seats, waiting for our check. Everyone was getting along like it was an episode of a Disney Channel sitcom. Kase propped his arm on the back of my chair around me and leaned in close to ask me a question.

"Do you have a request for the jukebox?"

"Mr. Moonlight."

Before Kase dismissed himself, I kissed his cheek. Then he walked over to the old-fashioned record player and dropped a couple quarters in the slot.

Marcel cleared his throat and asked, "Is that your nickname for him? Or am I missing something?"

"It's the name of an old Beatles song. I guess you could say it's our song."

"From what your father told my mother, he's under the impression that it *was* your song," Marcel said with a hint of accusation. He'd remained perfectly casual, but I could tell he didn't like being out of the loop.

In fact, everyone had frozen in place, and I wasn't sure if it was because of Marcel's observation or because they were all wondering too. Kase and I had barely discussed getting back together, and I felt the need in that moment to defend my love for him. Because I knew it was love, and not the silly infatuation I'd felt for Marcel's brother, Armand.

My mouth started to open, and Kase's hand squeezed my shoulder. His touch calmed me. When I first met him, I thought he was a jerk, like his girlfriend at the time, Ana. He'd used the rest of our junior year to prove me wrong.

"If you came here because of something my father said, you've come a long way for nothing." My mind raced trying to think of another reason he'd be here.

Marcel crossed one leg over the other, toward me, and retorted, "My visit was orchestrated by our parents, but I came for my own reasons. I think it's nice you have someone in your life."

He sounded genuine, but I couldn't help notice Willa's eyes narrow suspiciously. As she watched him, I could tell she was holding her tongue. So far, Marcel had been a little awkward, funny, and kind. He'd been the same Marcel I remembered from before I'd started dating his brother.

We all knew if we went on the defensive, we'd never figure out why Marcel was in Havenwood Falls, but I was starting to think he'd really come to apologize. As a group, we'd come up with a game plan earlier that morning, and we had to follow through.

"Hey, kiddos, I've got your check here," Maggie said as she skated to our table. She placed the ticket at the center of the table, and grabbed a few of the empty baskets. "You can square up with me whenever you're ready."

We all pulled out cash. My ten-dollar bill was crisp. Kase revealed a twenty and tossed it on the table.

"I've got yours," he offered.

Marcel started to pull his wallet out of his back pocket, and I held my hand up to stop him. "I'll pay for yours."

"You don't ha—" Marcel started to refuse.

"Don't argue, it's the least I can do."

He resigned and leaned back, watching the people around us.

"So, Marcel, if you've got reasons for being here, please share," Bale said flippantly, as he set a few fives in front of him. "But I should warn you, if skiing is on your list, you're out of luck. The season ended today."

Sometimes the dragon shifter amazed me; other times, I wanted to smack him in the back of the head. Most of the teenage guys I knew elicited those feelings, but Bale had a way of coming across as more sullen than all the rest.

"You can check *best burgers in town* off your list," Scarlet added with a smile and a shrug. She set some money on the table too.

"Relaxing, some hiking, and spending time catching up with Elle," Marcel listed out loud.

"We can take care of relaxing today. How about you come over and finish the movie marathon with us?" I invited hesitantly, but couldn't imagine Marcel's mother allowing him to read or watch anything Harry Potter. Her idea of raising children included piano lessons, a French tutor, and fencing practice.

"And we're going hiking Wednesday," Tarron said. Watching his face, I could tell he hadn't thought the remark through.

My head shook slightly, and I forced a smile. "Oh, Marcel won't enjoy the type of hiking we have planned. Three days is a long time, and I don't think he's ever been camping before."

Marcel's brows furrowed, and his eyes shifted from Tarron to me. His shoulders hunched forward enough that I could tell he was disappointed. I couldn't bring myself to ask him to join us, since the trip was for the Scooby Gang. They would argue it would be the best opportunity to get Marcel out of his comfort zone and talking.

Kase slipped his hand in mine and pulled me up to stand with him. With a gentle squeeze, he looked from me to Marcel and said, "If you've never been camping before, then we need to fix that. Mount Alexa is the most beautiful hike, and everyone should be able to say they've slept under the moon and stars at least once."

"When do we leave?" Marcel asked with a giddy grin as he stood.

"Wednesday." My heart sank as I confirmed the day. Getting down to the bottom of why he was in Havenwood Falls was one thing, but allowing him to intrude on our last trip together before graduating felt wrong. It was like Scooby and the gang taking a joy ride with Nate Archibald from *Gossip Girl*.

Willa made her way around the table and chimed in, "Kase, I forgot to ask, who'd you get to cover your shift Wednesday?"

Kase's mouth turned down for a split second, and he answered, "Joe."

"Is he doing any better?" Scarlet asked, and worry lines creased her forehead.

"Not that I can tell, but I figured work would keep his mind off things. And he'll be with Tate, so they might even have some fun." Kase's frown lightened.

Their older brother, Tate, was adventurous to say the least. The Kasun family had an interesting dynamic, since Willa would be alpha of their pack someday. Their oldest brother, Conall, was a clone of their father. And Kase was the perfect mix of all of them, fun and cautious. The weight of the family name and the expectations that came with it were a burden, but Kase never failed to be himself.

As we made our way to the exit, Marcel paused to carefully fold his milkshake-stained coat over his arm. Behind him, I noticed Ana and her crew getting up from their table. The compact blonde had a way of making herself seen, and today was no different. She saw Marcel and elbowed her partner in crime, Marie. When Marie's eyes widened at the sight of fresh meat, Ana quickly elbowed her in the side and let out a low growl.

"You must be new in town," she started, and turned her nose up. "I'm Ana Novak, and you are—"

Marcel, with impeccable manners, held out his hand and said, "Marcel. It's a pleasure to meet you, Ana."

The varsity mean girl glanced over at the rest of us, her top lip curled up when she looked back at Marcel. "You are definitely not from around here, but that doesn't change the fact that you're not my type." Ana pressed her finger to Marcel's chest, and added, "It's too bad for you my dating policy only includes guys with a beating heart."

One corner of Marcel's mouth twitched upward, giving him away. He liked the attention from Ana, and maybe the challenge, but it made me want to barf. There wasn't a jealous bone in my body when it came to Marcel. Since I'd learned that Ana had been behind a plot to steal Willa's position as alpha last year, I'd wanted to teach her a lesson. But Willa and Scarlet assured me she'd get what she deserved one day.

"Hey," Bale called over to Marcel, "we're headed to Elle's house. I promised Tarron we'd finish these movies. You coming?"

Marcel looked from us to Ana and winked at her teasingly. She looked over at me in disgust and flipped her hair over her shoulder before walking away.

Marcel said, "I'll be right behind you guys."

CHAPTER 8

KASE

*W*ednesday morning was cold. I woke up early and loaded my truck with three days of supplies. The night before, the girls had insisted on including the makings for hot dogs and s'mores, but I'd refused to pack air mattresses. The weather promised to be clear, and if everything went according to plan, I'd have a surprise for everyone when we reached the top of our climb.

Before leaving the cabin, my dad warned Willa and me there was to be no funny business. He sternly requested we stick to the hike we'd discussed. We both nodded, and he winked at me. Willa wasn't in on the scheme, but I'd enlisted my dad's and Tate's help.

As my sister and I pulled up to Elle's house, the others were gathering their packs into a pile at the end of the driveway. While parking, I rolled my window down and called, "Good morning!"

Bale glared at me in disgust and asked, "How are you a morning person and a night person?"

"I'm just excited. This camping trip is going to be epic."

After the movie marathon Monday—and into early Tuesday morning—we'd all gone home late—or early. Tuesday meant work for most of us. Willa and I manned Backwoods, Scarlet had a shift at Howe's Herbal Shoppe, Bale was working on his motorcycle, and Elle spent the morning trying to get ahold of her parents. On my lunch break, she and I met at Coffee Haven, and she told me she was only able to get in touch with her mother.

Mrs. Martin promised she and her husband would be back in Havenwood Falls by the time we returned from camping on Friday, but she hadn't been included in the plans for Marcel's visit. Because Elle hadn't talked to her father, Mrs. Martin reasoned he must have set it up. Supposedly, Elle's parents had important jobs in New York City, and it sounded like their jobs took precedence. They hadn't seen each other much on their trip. If I moved there for college, I hoped Elle and I would still make it a priority to spend time together.

"Kase, please don't be mad," Elle said, tearing me away from my thoughts. Her bottom lip pouted out. "But I packed one more teeny, tiny bag with some extra food."

She made it impossible to be upset with her, and curiosity got the best of me. "What all did you add?"

She walked up to my door, pushed up onto her toes, and kissed my cheek. Then she said, "Popcorn, apple juice, cinnamon sticks, and icing."

"Icing?" I asked with my head tilted.

"Whipped milk chocolate, if I'm not mistaken," Marcel confidently predicted.

"No, I know which kind she likes. I'm just surprised she needs it for camping."

"You never know what you'll need," she countered and kissed me on the cheek again.

I grinned from ear to ear.

"Marcel helped me shop yesterday," she said softly, and winked at me. I glanced over at Marcel, and his eyes were on me. He wore a smirk, but I couldn't tell what he meant by it. He quickly took his phone out of his coat pocket and proceeded to type something out.

Yesterday afternoon, while we each worked a second shift, Elle gave Marcel a tour of the town. My skepticism was difficult to hide when he'd called during our lunch date, but Elle mistook it for being worried about my friend, Joe. And I was concerned, because he'd shown up at Coffee Haven and appeared distraught. When I tried approaching him to settle our differences, he wouldn't stay to hear me out. Joe almost came across as angry at Elle when she added that she missed seeing him. The encounter led me to text my dad about Joe. And while we were camping, my dad promised to confront Joe.

Before I left Elle to go back to work, she revealed she had some reservations about being alone with Marcel that afternoon. We came up with a few ways she could make sure they stayed in the public eye. And last night, after we listed out everything we each needed to pack, Elle told me and the others that Marcel was a gentleman all afternoon.

"Don't forget, whatever we take, we're carrying up the mountain." Opening my door, I stepped down from the driver's seat. Patting the side of the truck, I added, "We should be able to fit everything back here."

Willa walked around from the passenger side and assured, "Tate should be here in a few minutes."

"Oh, is someone else joining us?" Marcel asked, and loaded his backpack into the bed of the truck.

"Our older brother is just helping with transportation," Willa informed. "He knows these forests better than anyone, and his Jeep can handle the muddy terrain better than Tarron's or Elle's cars."

Marcel nodded his understanding and stepped out of the way as Bale lifted Scarlet's bag. Once everything was loaded, Tate arrived. He steered with a hand full of pastry, and after he shifted his vehicle into park, he took a swig from a Coffee Haven cup.

Not long after Elle and I started dating last summer, my brother settled into a relationship of his own. Tate and Alex were perfect for each other. They were both adventurous, and where Tate lacked organizational skills and focus, Alex made up for it. They complemented each other. The difference between my feelings for Elle and Tate's for Alex was Tate had experienced a magical connection to Alex. He'd found his mate.

"Who's riding with me?" Tate asked from inside his Jeep, unwilling to expose himself or his coffee to the cold.

Elle surveyed the group as they moved around each other to load the truck. As I shoved Tarron's bedroll into a corner, I noticed Marcel scrolling through his phone again. There was no way he'd get service while we were in the forest, so I didn't blame him for wanting to send a text or two. Anyone I would have wanted to check in with, other than Joe, was right here.

"Let's see," Elle reluctantly started. "How about Tarron, Willa, and Marcel? The drive won't be long, since we're hiking up the mountain."

No one argued with the arrangement, and just as we were piling into the truck, Tate stopped Elle. "Do you want to leave a house key with me? I'd be happy to keep an eye on the place since your parents are out of town."

"Oh, I think it'll be—" Elle started, looking confused.

Nodding, I offered my opinion, "That's a good idea."

Getting keys to Elle's place was crucial to my plan, and Tate and I had agreed asking for them at the last minute and taking her off guard would be the best way to keep the surprise a secret.

"Okay." She shrugged and handed her keys to him through his window.

Elle and I walked over to my truck, where Bale and Scarlet were already strapped in, and we took off on our adventure.

Hiking up Mount Alexa was a test of endurance and patience. Being a group of supernaturals, conquering the physical challenge came naturally. The first couple hours went smoothly, but then we had to make multiple stops for food and bathroom breaks. We took our time, to keep everyone happy, and finally reached the peak of the ridge we'd planned to set up camp late in the afternoon.

"Where do you guys want to set up the tents?" Marcel asked with eagerness. He slid his pack off his back and onto the ground.

"It'll be more important to find some dry wood and get a fire started," Willa informed, and crossed her arms over her chest.

Taking Elle's pack, I set it next to mine, and offered, "We'll look for the wood."

She smiled at me, and it was all the thanks I needed.

"Okay." Willa tapped her chin with a finger, then pointed at Marcel. "How about you find some rocks? We'll need to create a rock circle around the campfire."

Marcel fidgeted with his bag and offered a tight smile. "Since I'm new at all this, and don't know my way around the forest, how about I go with Elle?"

Willa glanced at me, and I gave her a lopsided grin, and said, "Feel free to join us."

The guy hadn't left Elle's side during our hike, and I could tell Willa noticed too. But I was determined not to let Marcel Cushing ruin our trip. It was his first time camping, and the concrete jungle he came from was very different from our forest. Willa assigned the stone-gathering to Scarlet and Bale, while she and Tarron went to fill our water bottles. There were several streams and creeks that threaded through the area.

Marcel talked nonstop about all the places he wanted to take Elle when she moved back to New York. He wouldn't let me get a word in. Marcel knew the trip was about all of us spending time together before we graduated, but he seemed determined to make sure no one else could get close to Elle.

"I'll even go with you to Central Park, so you can scout out which tree you would want to bond with," he rambled.

"*Want* to bond with?" Elle asked, and froze under an aspen tree. "You make it sound like I get to pick the tree."

"You know what I mean, Elle," he backtracked in a soft tone. "You'll find the tree you're meant to bond with, and you'll want to protect it."

"I guess you're right," she conceded. "My mother has always said something similar. I just wish I could talk to another dryad, and ask them about how they handled 'choosing.'" Elle held up her hands and made air quotes.

"I think that's a great idea." My eyebrows rose in approval. Seeing Elle among the towering trees, I knew it was where she belonged. She'd become as strong as the oldest pine trees in the forest, and her power rivaled the currents of the Colorado River.

Marcel frowned and said gruffly, "Mrs. Martin has been a dryad for hundreds of years. I'm sure she's told you all you need to know."

Picking up another dry branch, I avoided an argument. Ever since I'd known Elle, her parents had filled her head with their expectations of her. Some of their ideas for Elle's future even conflicted with each other. Because Elle was a hybrid, I believed she was capable of so much more than they knew.

My arms were full, and it was time we headed back to camp. Inspecting the area around us, I noticed Elle carrying a few twigs, but Marcel's hands were empty. We were surrounded by spruce and fir trees, all covered in green needles. It would be easy for anyone to get turned around out here. Luckily, I'd been running the perimeter of Havenwood Falls for years on patrol.

I asked, "Elle, do you know which way it is back to camp?"

We'd been wandering, and I was curious if she'd been paying attention.

Marcel took a step to the right, pointed, and answered, "This way, right?"

Ugh. He wouldn't even let Elle answer my question, so I'd have to find a way to ditch him. The key would be to play to his own lack of desire to lift a finger to do manual labor.

"You're right, so do you want to take this load back or collect some more branches?"

Marcel looked from me to Elle like he was searching for the correct answer, but there wasn't one. I was too smart for that.

"I think I'll take your load back," he said with a smug smile. "Elle and I can get the fire started, and you can pick up some extra wood."

"Actually, this doesn't weigh that much," I countered. "I bet you're strong enough to handle my load and the pieces Elle has."

"O-oh," he stuttered, and his nose wrinkled in confusion. "Of course I can handle it, but—"

"Great," Elle cut him off, catching on to my motives. "Then I can grab a few more branches too. You never know if we'll need them, and it's better to be safe than sorry."

Marcel didn't attempt to argue with Elle, and we piled the wood in his open arms. He started walking back to camp and disappeared from view about twenty feet away. Finally, Elle and I had some time alone.

Approaching her with a knowing smile, I slipped my hand into hers and pulled her toward a stream I knew flowed nearby. The warmth I felt in my heart knowing Elle wanted to be with me made me forget the cold air that left the tip of my nose numb. Our steps were in unison, and with it being late afternoon, we couldn't be away for long. It would be getting dark soon, and my surprise would be arriving soon.

As we moved out to a clearing near the stream, I turned to face Elle. Behind her, I thought I spotted a wolf. A striking white wolf from the Kasun pack—Joe. If I'd been in wolf form, I could have communicated with him. But he bound off farther into the forest before I had time to alert Elle.

"Do you want to go after him?" she asked softly, with a concerned frown.

"Nah, I'll check in on him when we get back Friday. I think he's missing Infiniti, and only time is going to mend his broken heart." I walked backwards and asked, "Are you doing okay?"

"I'm better now that we have a little time alone," she admitted with a relieved smile. "Being with you always makes me feel better."

Elle moved closer to me. I wrapped my arms around her waist and whispered, "You make me better."

We leaned into each other, and my lips met hers. As I kissed her, I allowed my heart and mind to open to her. Thoughts of a life with her and the love overflowing from me made her pause. Elle's lips brushed against mine as she murmured, "I love you, too."

The time away from the group was just what we needed before returning to the chaos Elle and I walked up on. Bale faced Marcel with a stone in each hand, and Marcel held a tree branch like a baseball bat. Bale was breathing smoke, but not because it was cold outside. Marcel's top lip curled up over his fangs.

"The stones first," Bale growled.

Marcel hissed, "Stacking the wood goes first."

"Dude, chill," Tarron said softly with his two arms outstretched between them. Tarron had the power to persuade if he wanted, but I knew it was a power he didn't like to use. From what I understood, persuasion on a supernatural level could have crazy side effects.

Dropping my load of branches, I distracted Marcel. He saw Elle at my side and immediately shuffled back from his confrontation with Bale, then said, "Whatever, dragon. I'm going to work on putting up my tent."

Marcel dropped his branch and walked away. When Willa asked if he needed any help, he ignored her. The guy had been fine with Elle around, but without her nearby, his attitude had the potential to ruin my plans tonight. So I'd have to stroke some egos.

"Bale, do you mind finishing while I go check on him?" He was the best candidate to get the fire started. He could breathe fire.

"Nah, go on," he said coolly and waved me away.

Marcel sighed when I reached him, and said, "I don't need you to come over here and tell me what an idiot I am."

"I wasn't going to. I wanted to let you know that Bale can come across strong sometimes. And that you don't need to set up your tent yet."

Marcel tilted his head to the side.

"Thing is, we're not staying here for long." Marcel didn't say anything, so I added, "After we eat, I have a surprise for everyone."

"But I'll need my tent eventually, and I'd rather assemble it now, before it's dark," he reasoned thoughtfully. "It's my first time camping, and I don't want to look—"

"How about I promise to set it up for you later? That way you can come back over to the campfire and cook hot dogs with the rest of us." My proposition didn't make a ton of sense, but I could see Marcel's wheels were turning.

"Okay, but I still think it would be best if I kept my distance. At least from Bale," Marcel said cautiously.

It probably was a good idea for Marcel not to assert himself, but his ability to have an opinion about everything made that impossible. I patted his shoulder, my goal to form some semblance of friendship. He flinched, and any connection I thought I'd made snapped.

Marcel pouted while roasting his hot dog, then glowered at Elle when we made s'mores. His attention had become focused, like he'd made the decision to disregard the rest of us. His behavior felt familiar, like how Joe had started obsessing over finding Infiniti. Joe hadn't intended to hurt anyone, but pushing others away hurt everyone. I tried not to make a big deal about it, because there were too many things for me to remember tonight.

First, I had to make sure it didn't seem odd when I suggested everyone go on a night hike. Second, timing was everything. If we left too early, it wouldn't give Tate enough time to set everything up. Lastly, the night needed to be perfect for Elle.

So when the girls started to complain about having sticky marshmallow fingers, I mentioned taking a walk to a nearby stream to rinse them off. Of course, the guys couldn't let them go alone, so I condensed a few things into one pack in case of an accident. We strapped headlamps to our foreheads. And then everyone was hiking at night without any suspicion.

Once we were approaching the spot Tate and I had agreed on, I knew Willa would get suspicious. She hadn't patrolled as many years as I had, but she'd been raised in these forests just the same. Tate waited to drive us out to the town border. He pulled up in the pickup and didn't say a word. We all piled into the back, and as we approached the enchanted border, Willa's mental warning bells went off. I could tell when her eyes grew wide. She understood I was leading my friends to come close to crossing it, but the area we were headed provided the best views. All my life, we'd been taught to keep the good in and drive the bad out.

I leaned over to Willa, and whispered, "Trust me."

She did.

As we cleared the thickest part of the forest, I spotted the lights Tate left behind in an open field. A campfire had been started several yards away in the distance. Two large tents were set up, one for the girls and the other for the boys. Lanterns were lit inside them, and they glowed green and orange. Between the tents, Elle's telescope stood, pointed at the sky. A few blankets were folded and stacked at its base.

"What is all this?" Elle asked from beside me.

"I thought stargazing would be fun, and I figured I could teach you the proper angle to use when looking through your telescope." A chuckle escaped me.

Elle laughed, then said, "This is perfect."

Tate had really outdone himself. He stopped the truck, and we all jumped out. With a wave and a honk, Tate headed back to town. He'd return the next morning.

Near the campfire we found the kit for making hot chocolate and tea that I'd arranged. The tin cups reminded me of the ones we had in our cabinets at home. Willa and Tarron were the first to grab a blanket and lay it over the ground.

As they stretched out, Willa asked, "How'd you make this happen?"

"Let's just say I'll be covering patrols for Tate for the unforeseeable future. Dad pulled a few strings with the Court since we're so close to the border. And if anyone asks, it's all for a science project." My laughter became uncontrollable at the thought of any of the Court members falling for the story.

Bale and Scarlet followed Willa and Tarron's example. Like me, Willa knew all the constellations and pointed them out to Tarron. Bale was doing something similar with Scarlet, but the stories he told about the stars were filled with more dragon history. Being dragon shifters, his ancestors had their own stories about how the sky became filled with fire and lights.

Past Elle, I watched as Marcel prepared to boil water in the kettle. At least he'd made himself busy. It was a beautiful night, even if it was cold. We were all bundled up, but a hot cup of tea would help warm us from the inside.

Elle and I made our way to the telescope, and she looked through the lens first. If Tate had followed my instructions to the letter, Elle would be looking at the moon. As she pulled away, her eyes widened with wonder.

I definitely owed Tate big time.

"Thank you," Elle said sweetly, and she pulled me to her and gave me a soft kiss.

Looking into her eyes, I said, "I promised you the moon, and I'll always keep my promises."

CHAPTER 9

ELLE

Jostled out of a deep sleep, I had no control of my body. Someone was carrying me over their shoulder and running. Everything was black, and I couldn't tell if my eyes were still closed or if it was the darkness of night. The sound of boots hitting the ground and the scent of sweet apricot surrounded us.

"To have seen her now unseen, to fade her now evade," a deep voice whispered, then repeated over and over, "To have seen her now unseen, to fade her now evade."

The words felt familiar, but I couldn't place them. My brain was foggy, and my breath tasted awful. The urge to check my surroundings nearly outweighed my desire to know who carried me. It had to be a man, because his shoulder was broad enough to throw me over it, and the steps he took made me feel like I was dangling high up from the ground.

The smell of herbs and my muddled mind made it difficult to place the man.

"To have seen her now unseen, to fade her now evade," he continued to chant. His movement was fluid, supernatural, and he moved around the forest swiftly, like someone who knew the area. Could it be Joe carrying me? Was he in so much pain over Infiniti's leaving that he'd try to keep me from Kase? I couldn't believe it.

My predicament was bad, but I wouldn't panic. The longer the guy, whoever it was, thought I was still asleep, the longer I had to come up with a plan. The vampire side of me wanted to attack, but I needed to keep myself in check. I'd never bitten anyone before, and being a dryad hybrid had allowed me to live a life sustained by food any human would eat. Even so, I'd choose steak over vegetables or fruit any day. Most vamps in New York succumbed to the temptation of bloodlust, but used their desire for power as an excuse to take advantage of humans. I wouldn't allow myself to lose control like them.

My father was different. He'd risen to power because of his ability to control his bloodlust. He'd been the only vampire to ever love a nymph or fae without losing control. He and my mother were great leaders because of their determination to live life following their hearts instead of the social expectations.

"To have seen her now unseen, to fade her now evade," the man said a little louder.

Pushing my supernatural senses outward, I took in a slow deep breath and listened for a heartbeat. A metallic scent filled my nose first, then my tastebuds tingled. The blood smelled old and rotten, like someone was dead. The sound of pounding feet filled my ears, matching my own racing heart, but there was no echo of another heartbeat.

That's when I knew: Marcel Cushing had kidnapped me.

The longer he ran, the clearer my thoughts became, and the farther we would be from the others. I had no way of knowing what time he'd grabbed me or how long we'd been gone, so I waited.

The terrain was uneven and with my powers extended around me, I could tell we were still surrounded by trees. Every now and then, tree limbs brushed over the fabric of my pants and coat. Being under the cover of trees made it seem darker, and if Marcel gave me and the others something to knock us out, there would have been no way to tell how late or early it was. Unless I could look up at the sky.

Kase had taught me a little about how to tell time using the stars and the moon while we admired the view from my telescope. It was difficult to imagine Marcel could take me from my friends without them hearing something. We were all supernaturals. Willa and Kase had super hearing, Bale's strength was impressive, Tarron had the ability to persuade, and Scarlet could cast spells and charms.

What if one of them heard a commotion? Or what if Marcel had made sure none of my friends could follow us? Impossible. Marcel may have been attention-hungry, but he hadn't said or done anything that made me think he was capable of violence.

My stomach turned, and my body seized, betraying me. We all suspected something was off about Marcel, and by inviting him to join us, I might have gotten them all killed.

Gasping, I pictured my friends—and my boyfriend—dead.

Marcel jerked to a stop. "Elle, I'm going to set you down, but don't try anything," he warned in a calm voice, like he was trying to talk me down from a ledge.

The forest's noises became deafening when I didn't respond. A breeze filled the air with the scent of pine and a rustling sound of needles brushing against each other. Creatures stirred in the trees, scurrying up and down branches. I could even hear the sound of water flowing in the distance.

"W-where are we?" My voice wavered, but I tried not to sound panicked.

"All you need to know is that we aren't in Havenwood Falls anymore," he answered and gently slid me off his shoulder and set me on the ground.

He wore a satisfied sneer.

My legs felt wobbly and weak, but I fought the urge to grab hold of something. The last thing I wanted was to come across as weak. I reached with my power, through my legs, into the ground for support. While the earth braced me and replenished my strength, I knew I needed to keep him talking.

I asked, "How?"

"Your adorable boyfriend and his family worked it all out for me," Marcel said arrogantly. "I'd prepared to put up a bigger fight, but when he surprised us all with front-row seats to the town's border, I knew the Court wouldn't give any notice to a blip on the supernatural radar."

Marcel Cushing wasn't the same little brother eager to please I remembered. We'd both changed, but I was afraid of who he'd become. Kase had set up an unforgettable night, and if someone in town felt a disturbance in the wards protecting Havenwood Falls, they might have dismissed it. No one would suspect anything until Friday. Our families expected us to be back Friday afternoon, but none of us would show up.

"Are the others—" My mouth wouldn't form the word *dead*.

Marcel's eyebrows pulled together, and his eyes narrowed. His lips pressed together, then he said, "You think I could do something like that?"

"I don't know." My voice came out raspy, and I was sure I'd struck a nerve. "I didn't think you could do *this*." My hand waved in front of me, motioning at where we stood.

"I did *this* for us," he said, sounding surprised that I didn't understand.

"F-for us, Marcel? What all did you do? How did you find me?" Something clicked for me in that moment, and the thought of my father sending Marcel to Havenwood Falls suddenly seemed absurd.

Marcel gritted his teeth together and took a deep breath through his nose, then he said, "Your stupid friends aren't dead, unless one of them is allergic to valerian."

My relief came out in a sigh. We'd all been drugged with a powerful sleeping herb. They would sleep through the night, so I had to think of a way to leave them clues. My pause sparked more anger from Marcel.

"There's no way they'll find us," he promised. "At least not before we get to New York. Then you won't want to come back here."

What Marcel said didn't make sense. Asking more questions would only make him angrier, so I decided to take a different approach. Marcel's family had become accustomed to other vampire clans stroking their ego over the years. The thirst for power burned as strongly as the thirst for blood in my father's world.

"You know, if you'd waited a few more months, you wouldn't have had to go to all this trouble." My mouth pulled into a tight smile.

Marcel's mouth spread into a wide smile, and he said, "Waited? I've never waited for you. Since the night I killed my brother, I've been searching for—no, hunting—you. When I killed Armand that night, I got a taste for what he was after. He was only pretending to join our bloodlines, but where he was weak, I'll be strong. I won't lose control like he did."

What he referred to was my deepest fear. My blood had the power to make vampires go mad, and it wasn't until I'd gotten too close to Marcel's brother that I found out the lengths a vampire would go to to get it. Armand hadn't even kissed me, and I knew something was terribly wrong. In my struggle to keep him from biting me, I was scratched. His thirst took over, and he was stronger than anyone I'd ever known. If it hadn't been for Marcel, I would have died that night.

"You saved me two years ago," I whispered. "But you're not saving me now."

Marcel may have thought he was strong enough to withstand the temptation of my blood, but after he killed his brother, I was swept away to Colorado. Because he'd been exposed to the scent of my blood, I wondered if it had been torturing him since then. If so, Marcel wouldn't be able to accept that I didn't want to be with him, or any vampire.

"That's where you're wrong," he growled. "Your parents have kept you from the best our world has to offer. I could give you everything you ever wanted. Your middle-class mutt can't offer you an eternity like I can. I'm saving you and me."

"What do you mean saving you?"

"Our family was shunned after word got out about Armand losing control. Your father exposed my mother as the mastermind, and I've been on the run since. With you at my side, I can restore the Cushing name and lead the New York clans to a new way of regulating the supernaturals in the area. Discovering Havenwood Falls was an accident, and the Court is on to something, but they aren't seeing the full potential. You're lucky I love you."

"If you really loved me, wouldn't you let me decide my own future?" Marcel's train of thought confused me. He only understood obsession.

"Love is making the hard choices," Marcel said flatly. "And let's be honest, the decisions you've made for yourself here are questionable.

With Kase, you're weak, but with me you'd be the strongest you've ever been. The hybrid blood flowing in your veins needs to feed off a superior bloodline."

My mouth fell open.

Heat rose in my chest, up my neck, and into my cheeks. Something carnal inside me wanted to be released and let loose on Marcel. Squeezing my hands into fists, I was determined to stay in control. Channeling my physical strength into the ground under my feet, I released power instead of pulling it, and the earth vibrated. The sensation shocked and scared me, as well as Marcel.

Even though the power that left me felt chaotic and vengeful, it rippled back toward me and gave me a sense of peace. I knew the comfort I received came from someone else in the forest. But who?

"What did you just do?" Marcel asked in rage.

"I don't know. It was a first."

Marcel reached into his pocket, pulled out his fist, and said, "Well, I can't risk that happening again."

He opened his hand and blew a cloud of silvery dust into my face. It was the last thing I saw until sunrise.

Slowly, I regained consciousness, but I was hanging over Marcel's shoulder again. Careful not to move any other part of my body, I opened my eyes to survey the ground. It didn't look any different from any other forest floor.

Extending my supernatural powers outside of myself, I could hear rushing water, but there weren't any minds nearby I could read. My sense of smell picked up on a few rodents in the vicinity, maybe squirrels. But the sound of the stream was consistent, and eventually made me thirsty.

"Marcel?" My voice feigned grogginess.

It was light out, but until I saw the sun's position in the sky, I wouldn't be able to approximate the time. There was no way to know if the others would wake up with the new day or if the valerian would keep them sleeping through noon. Since Marcel bought it from

Howe's Herbal Shoppe, I figured Ruby added a charm or spell to increase its power. Until I woke up slung over Marcel's shoulder, I had thought there'd been a possibility Joe bought it.

"Marcel," I said louder, when he hadn't slowed down. "I'm thirsty."

He kept walking at a steady pace, unfazed, and asked, "Thirsty for what?"

"Water."

Marcel turned right and took about twenty paces before letting me down next to the stream I'd heard. Kneeling down at its edge, I scooped water to my mouth with my hands. It was cold and refreshing. To help wake myself up, I splashed one handful of water on my face. Then, dipping my hands in the water, I tried to replicate the power I'd sent into the ground by mistake. The force I emitted fizzled in comparison.

"Okay, let's get moving," Marcel ordered impatiently.

"Can't we rest a few more minutes? You have to be tired, and I would love a snack, if you have one."

"If you'd drink from me, you could not only be sustained, but your powers would be strengthened by my bloodline. You'd be unstoppable, and I'd never leave your side," Marcel said as he knelt down beside me.

"That's not what I want. It's what you want. You're not fooling anyone. I know you want to feed on me," I spat, and in my peripheral vision, I caught a flash of white fur in the distance. Before I could call out, I felt something collide with my chin.

This time, it wasn't a powder or spell that knocked me unconscious, but Marcel's fist.

CHAPTER 10

KASE

Thursday morning I woke up in a haze. The amount of light shining through the tents' orange walls made them appear neon. My dreams had been filled with scenes of Elle and me in New York together. Closing my eyes, I attempted to fall back into my dreamland, but a shadow caught my attention as it moved quickly across the far wall.

"Kase?" Willa called softly, from outside the tent.

Unzipping my sleeping bag and then the front flap of the tent, I crawled out. "Hey, are you okay?"

"I'm fine, but when I woke up, Elle wasn't in our tent. I thought I'd check to see if you were with her," she explained.

Surveying the area around camp, I didn't see anyone, but I told myself it didn't mean she wasn't out exploring. My mind felt like it was full and empty at the same time, so I shook my head. With one hand, I lifted our tent's flap and counted sleeping bags. We were missing one. I looked back at Willa, and her eyes were wide with worry.

"I have a really bad feeling," she said ominously.

"Go wake Scarlet up, and I'll get the guys."

We all met back at the center of camp in less than three minutes. Tarron yawned into his elbow, probably hiding his morning breath.

Scarlet scowled at everyone, but she'd never been much of a morning person. Bale rubbed his forehead like he had a headache.

We'd stayed up late the night before, but other than seeing Joe in the distance again, nothing had felt off. There weren't any more weird vibes coming from Marcel. I didn't think he would hurt Elle, and I naively kept telling myself they could be scouting the area.

"Elle never really sleeps through the night," Willa reasoned with a forced smile.

"You're right," Scarlet agreed in a monotone voice. "But we're *never really* drugged, either."

"Is that why my head feels like a snow globe a kid's shaken too much?" Bale asked and pressed his hands to his ears.

"Yeah," she answered and smacked her lips. "The aftertaste makes me think it was valerian, and the effects it's having leads me to believe it's the same charmed order I saw in my grandmother's ledger."

"He must have put it in the drinks last night," Bale guessed while picking up his backpack.

"The hot chocolate would have hidden the scent and flavor of the valerian, and if Marcel wanted to get as far as possible, he would have left right after we all fell asleep," Scarlet explained.

"He would have drugged her too. There's no way she'd go with him alone," I said through gritted teeth, and began to pace. "At this rate on foot, they could be ten to twenty miles away. And I gave Marcel the perfect opportunity to get a head start."

"You can't blame yourself," Willa consoled. "But you can go find her."

"You're right. Without a cell signal, you'll have to shift and run back to town to tell Dad. You're the fastest."

Bale cleared his throat, and Willa added, "I'm the fastest who won't scare the crap out of tourists if they see me running through the forest."

"Accurate," he said with a nod.

In wolf form, Willa could get to town and risk being seen by the public. As a dragon running down Main Street, Bale would put the supernatural community in jeopardy. There have been some wild stories told by humans in town, but they'd been diluted into rumors and legends.

Willa didn't excuse herself and take the time to undress, but shifted out in the open. Her clothes ripped to shreds as her body supernaturally morphed into a black wolf with golden eyes. Before the shimmering magic disappeared, she'd taken off at full speed, back the way we'd come the night before.

"So we'll need to split up if we want to cover more area. Scarlet, will you go with Bale?" I asked.

Scarlet scoffed at me, and said, "I can search by myself if we need to cover more area. I'm not scared of anything in this forest."

"I don't doubt that, but I need someone to calm Bale down in case he's the one who finds Marcel. I want to wring Marcel's neck, and Tarron will go with me to keep me calm."

"Which way do you want us to head?" Bale asked, and strapped his backpack on.

Peering into the forest, I had a gut feeling, so I told him, "Northwest. Anywhere south of us will be deeper within the town's borders. Fanning out northward will be our best bet of picking up their scent."

"Got it." Bale nodded, then met my eyes. "If we find them, there's a 99% chance we won't have cell reception. How do you want me to—"

"I want you to save Elle, period," I gritted out, and my chest pounded anxiously. "If you have to shift and airlift her and Scarlet, do it. It's less likely someone will see a dragon out there, and if they do, we'll take care of them after Elle is safe."

"My mom has cast memory charms on a few of the citizens of Havenwood Falls," Scarlet pointed out. "All Court-approved, of course."

"Okay, if you don't find them or pick up their scent in two to three hours, start heading back here. If one of us doesn't show up, then we can assume the other is tailing Elle and Marcel." Grabbing my own backpack, I slipped it on.

We started walking toward the forest at the far edge of the field. The closer we got to the tree line, the farther away we veered from each other in an effort to cover more ground. The spring day would be shorter than a summer day, so we'd need to move fast. Once Tarron and I reached the cover of a towering pine tree, he stopped.

"Give me the pack," Tarron ordered with a somber tone. "I'll only hold you back, and if you're in your wolf form, you can use all of your powers to find her. I promise to keep moving, and I won't be too far behind."

"Are you sure?"

But he was right. If anything happened to Elle because I'd been a second too slow, I'd blame myself, and maybe everyone else, too.

"Go," he insisted.

Shifting mid-stride into a black wolf, I ran faster than I'd ever run before.

CHAPTER 11

ELLE

*T*he taste of coppery, tangy blood was the first thing I noticed when I woke. Licking along my bottom lip, I found one side swelled, as if I'd tucked a gumball behind it. The second thing I noticed was rocky ground underneath me, but I wasn't outside. Darkness loomed around me. It was as if the sun, moon, and stars had blinked out of existence. My ability to see in the dark didn't come in handy, because there wasn't anything or anyone that I could see. Stone walls surrounded me.

"Hello?" I whispered, and my voice echoed, like I was in a cave. "M-M-Marcel," I called a little louder, pushing past my fear. Had I been buried alive?

The idea of Marcel entering the room scared me, but the thought of being left in a tomb of sorts without a way out terrified me more. There was no way to tell how long I'd been unconscious until I made it outside.

When I pushed myself up from the ground, my muscles groaned in protest. My neck especially felt sore, and when I rubbed from my hairline to my throat I understood why. Two small scars, one next to the other, marked where someone had punctured my carotid artery. In a moment, I went from being thankful I hadn't been killed to being angry Marcel had taken my blood without consent. Searching the cavern for an exit, I noticed an overlap of rock along one of the walls.

"Stay there," a raspy voice ordered. It had to be Marcel, but I couldn't see him.

Vampires had a reputation on television for not caring about where they acquired their life source. In movies, bloodsuckers were charming murderers or glittering celebrity crushes. But in the social circles my father had been raised in, it was crucial to maintain a pure bloodline. A vampire only sired a human worthy of their name, unless they didn't have control of their bloodlust. Then, once turned, they fed on supernaturals.

My father's influence in New York came from being remarkably disciplined. Most vampires survived by more base desires. His clan had elected him leader because he earned the love and consent of a dryad. With my mother as his life source, my father did gain a vitality other vampires longed for, but he saw it as a gift. Feeding on a supernatural against their will had serious consequences, physically and emotionally.

"Why?" My voice croaked as tears streamed down my cheeks, not in fear, but in shame. Why hadn't I fought him earlier? Maybe I could have escaped.

"I don't have to answer to you," he snapped in anger, and began chanting, "To have seen her now unseen, to fade her now evade."

The sweet scent of herbs filled the cavern, and the sound of his voice bounced off the walls differently than mine. While he was distracted, my hands reached for the wall closest to me, and I made my way around the room slowly until I came to an opening.

"Don't," he snarled. "If you try to leave, I won't be able to control myself. I'll hunt you until one of us is dead."

And there it was—the consequence.

The same way a human's taste grew into an addiction without boundaries, a vampire's taste ended in death without a mutual consent. When Marcel struck me, he'd probably tried to resist the scent of blood emanating from my lip, but eventually lost control.

Unsure if I even had the energy to fight back, I knelt down and tried to reach out magically through the stone floor. What power I had built up in my fingertips searched for life under the rock. Sensing a conduit, my power surged into the earth. The cave rumbled, and dust fell from the ceiling, except at the center of the room.

When the dust settled I looked up. Marcel clung to the ceiling with his hands unnaturally and skittered across the stone like an insect. He stopped above me and began to hum to himself. Spiderman movies would never be the same.

I ignored his tune and focused on the sound of my heartbeat until it filled my ears. Closing my eyes, I tried to center myself. I thought of Kase and the others. Like Kase was in the next room, I heard his thoughts call my name. *Elle.*

In that moment, I'd known my physical and mental strength were waning. I had to be hallucinating. If I stayed in the cave much longer, I would never be able to escape. Making a move soon would be the only chance I had. Once outside, I had a feeling I could find safety, but I'd have to outrun Marcel. With my supernatural blood flowing in his veins, Marcel's reactions and powers would be unpredictable.

"I know what you're thinking," Marcel's voice gritted in anger.

I shuddered.

He'd been able to read my mind since he'd tasted my blood. How could I have forgotten that? I'd never be able to get away from him.

"That's right," he hissed. "And now that you're conscious, we'll climb over this mountain and meet up with the transportation I've arranged."

"I can barely move around this room. How do you expect me to climb a mountain?" I argued, irritated.

Marcel let go of the wall and landed a few feet away from me. As he inhaled, his nostrils flared, his chest expanded, and a maniacal smile spread across his lips. His tongue swept over his fanged teeth.

"I would offer to carry you, but I'm afraid you'd prove too enticing at such a close distance. It was all I could do to stop myself before," he said with a laugh. "I don't want you dead. Eventually, I know I'll convince you to feed, but until then, I'll settle for you to be in a weakened state at my side. I can be patient."

Marcel's brother died trying to get a taste of my blood. I found myself curious, like someone drawn to look in the direction of a car crash, and asked, "How did you stop yourself?"

"Oh, I've been practicing for two years," he said as he crossed his arms over his chest and leaned against the cave wall. "That night you left, when my brother lost control, I fought to have you for myself. Your parents dragged you away, and I can't blame you for leaving with them, but you left a part of yourself with me."

"You did save me from Armand, and I'm thankful for that, but I never gave you the impression that we were anything more than friends. Why would you hold on to the idea that we were anything more?" My voice softened, trying to keep either of us from getting angry.

"No, you're not listening." His smile faded into a frown. "You are a chalice among coffee mugs. I've had a part of you with me every day we've been apart. Your injuries from two years ago left traces of blood at our home. Mother insisted on a deep cleaning, but I managed to steal away a piece of fabric with just enough of your blood to help me learn to control my bloodlust. During my search for you, I conditioned myself, making me stronger than my brother ever was. And I will drink from my chalice while the vampires who shunned me slurp from their mugs."

The pieces were slowly fitting together, but I didn't have the picture of the puzzle to refer to. Marcel must have been going mad trying to build up a tolerance to the scent of my blood since I moved to Havenwood Falls. He'd driven himself to this point. His search for me started as a crusade. He wanted me to choose him, but in the last two years, he'd become homicidal.

"So the only way out of here is with you."

"You're catching on." Marcel nodded, and his hand reached out to touch my face. I flinched, and he forced the issue and tucked my hair behind my ear. "The charm I'm using should hide us from your annoying friends. I'd hate to have to kill them, but I'm sure you'll cooperate so I don't have to resort to such violence."

And I would. I'd go wherever Marcel wanted to keep the others safe, but when he mentioned remembering my friends I suddenly realized we hadn't crossed the town's border. If we'd passed the wards,

Marcel wouldn't have been able to recall Havenwood Falls or anyone he met while visiting. If he'd gotten turned around in the forest, maybe there was still hope the others would find me.

Marcel took my hand and led me out of the cave. Surprised by the sight of stars in the sky, I focused on searching for the North Star. There was no way to tell exactly where we were, but I could figure out which direction we were headed. Unlike Kase, I hadn't grown up wandering these forests. The names of the different peaks and rock formations were lost on me.

"You must not let go," Marcel ordered. "The climb is steep, but as you've witnessed, I have enough strength from your blood to cling to anything. I won't let you fall."

His eyes gazed at me longingly, and I shivered. His bloodlust would never be satiated by me, or anyone for that matter. He'd given in to the darkest part of being a vampire. There was no way to tell if he'd be able to control himself the next time he decided to drink from me.

Marcel clenched his jaw in anger at hearing my thoughts.

"Let me make myself clear. If you do let go or make a run for it, I won't bother going after you. I'll find Kase and drink him until there's no life left in him."

After I nodded my understanding, he yanked me forward.

We were already a third of the way up the mountain when we passed a beautiful formation of aspen trees. Their bare branches waved at me as if saying goodbye. My heart ached at the thought of leaving these mountains. Then a feeling of calm came over me. The sadness wasn't gone, but something outside myself shared their confidence, their peace. I supernaturally knew everything would work out.

My eyes darted to Marcel, expecting him to respond to my thoughts, but he didn't. The thoughts and feelings being shared with me were from someone else out in the forest, and they were somehow protected. We were definitely still in Havenwood Falls.

Reach within and distract him.

The words were clear, but I had no clue who they were coming from. Like my doubt had been heard, the voice responded.

Trust me and flee.

So I started rambling. "How do you think my family will react to what you've done? You have to know my father will not be happy. And even if your mom put you up to this, like she did Armand, you can't explain away feeding on me without my consent."

Marcel stilled, and his grip on my hand tightened. It hurt. He turned to face me, and gave me a devilish grin. "Oh, my mother didn't have anything to do with this. She's grown complacent over the last year, alone. With you at my side, we'll take over leading a nest of our own, and eventually you'll convince your family to join us. Your parents don't need to know about our little mishap. It was your fault anyway. If you hadn't fallen for my brother, none of this would have happened. I had to kill him to protect you. I'll kill anyone who threatens to separate us."

His last words were a promise. Understanding he meant my friends, I took a step up the mountain in his direction.

Suddenly, a ball of light revealed itself ahead of us. It was bigger than a firefly, but smaller than a flashlight. Power emanated from the glowing source, and I instinctively knew it was the entity trying to help me. The problem was I didn't know if it wanted me to follow it or flee in the opposite direction.

Remembering Marcel's last words to me, I considered the direction we were headed. If he'd been telling the truth, he'd pursue whatever or whoever flickered in the distance. Before my thoughts could betray me, I bolted away from the light and Marcel.

My hand jerked out of his, and the magic hiding us shattered.

"Elle," he howled.

My legs struggled to stay under me. Running down the mountain, my upper body wanted to tumble forward as loose stones and rocks skittered underfoot. The sound of Marcel running faded behind me, and I pushed my worry for whoever saved me to the back of my mind. Marcel was jacked on my blood, and after he ripped whatever that light was to shreds, he'd come after me.

My best chance of escaping Marcel would be to get back to the Havenwood Falls border. Hopefully, the wards would trip and the Court would send reinforcements. The stars told me I was headed south when I glanced up, and the moon had almost rotated out of view. It was around midnight. The next thing I needed to listen for was water. It would be easier to follow the current to the town's waterfall, and the noise would muffle the sound of my boots pounding the ground.

It felt like I'd been running for hours when I finally found the babbling water. My heart, mind, and body raced.

～

The stream grew wider the farther I ran toward Havenwood Falls. Something supernatural called from ahead. Whether it was the town itself or the people in it, the desire to be home overwhelmed me. All the while, the thought of Marcel following me made my stomach turn. All I could do was push forward.

Rock formations and trees along the water's edge helped keep me hidden, but the sound of a twig breaking sent me scrambling for cover. I noticed a white wolf in the distance running on the other side of the water. Joe. He was too far away to have produced the noise. On my side of the river, two large bristlecone pines had a narrow opening where their twisted trunks entwined. Sliding into the crevasse, I pressed my hand against my mouth, trying to silence my breathing.

Oh my dear, do not fear. A singsong voice invaded my thoughts.

The thought was followed by a warm sense of peace. In the arms of the trees, I felt protected. I knew, because of my mother's dryad blood, I had a connection with the earth. Eventually, I'd bond with a tree and be connected more permanently.

We are of one kind, and of one mind. I want to help you, because we are so few. There is a place for you here, there is no reason for tears.

"Where are you?" Whispering, I dared to peek out of my hiding place.

A small light, the size of a luna moth, floated in the air around the tree.

"You are beautiful. Are you the one who helped me earlier?"

Your need called out to me.

"Thank you, but I don't understand how we are of one kind. There's no one like me."

We may be different in body, but our purpose is to protect all trees. Your heart is pure, but your mind unsure. The place of your true intention will also be your destination. Do not fret in this hiding place. You are safe.

And she had made me feel safe. Her calm, steady emotions flooded me. "Who are you?"

Cyllene, the oldest of our kind in this forest growth. Fading with my true love, soon rest will claim us both. Until then, I protect the worthy, both man and tree.

"Before, you mentioned my destination. Do you sense where I belong? I thought I had to go back to New York, but after tonight I'm not sure I'll ever want to. I don't know if we'll even survive. What would happen if I chose to stay in Havenwood Falls?"

Cyllene was constantly moving. She, and her light, were warm and inviting. Her grace and wisdom reminded me of my own mother, but Cyllene's presence felt ancient.

Born of blood and born of earth, your path has varied since your birth. Home is heart and heart is home. Roots will grow deep, there's no cause to roam. Follow your heart. Protect and guard, the trees are not your whole but part.

Her rhyming helped me remember her words, but they didn't help me interpret them. My life always felt like I was balancing on a tightrope, but I'd looked forward to bonding with a tree so I could feel rooted. Maybe the reason I'd been struggling to leave Havenwood Falls was because I shouldn't leave. My heart belonged to Kase, my friends, and this mountain.

"Elle!" Marcel's voice thundered from a distance, making me jump. My head bumped the underside of one of the trees.

"Can you feel how far away he is?" Panicked, I pulled myself out into the open and hoped Cyllene could tell me how much time I had before Marcel reached me.

You've reached the earth your heart longs for. No need to run, merely open the door.

"Thank you." My appreciation fell flat, because my fight-or-flight response was to run into the forest, away from Marcel.

Cyllene had told me I didn't have to run, but if he caught up with me, I feared I might not survive his wrath. My eyes searched the mountain for the door Cyllene mentioned, but there were only trees and boulders in sight. The river's current grew stronger, and a light mist filled the air. The spray was shockingly cold against my skin and coated my jacket with beads of water. The cool moisture made me feel alive, and I increased my pace.

The wet stone underfoot made it difficult to get traction, and I slipped. Falling face forward, my chin hit rock. My hands flung forward too late and scraped against the rock. The impact took my breath away.

When I shook my head, my jaw ached. Pushing up to get my feet underneath me, I glanced at the bank of the river and recognized the door Cyllene had referenced. It wasn't a plank of wood with a knob or a metal gate with a latch. A few feet in front of me, a majestic pine tree stood with its roots exposed. Some of the roots reached into the river, and it looked like the tree was dipping its toe in the water. The other roots spread over a boulder the size of Kase's truck. They reached through cracks in the rock for earth. One space between the roots appeared to be large enough for me to walk through, and the trunk above reached over fifty feet high with a canopy of limbs stretched over the river.

"Where do you think you're going?" Marcel spat from somewhere behind me.

"Leave me alone!" What I'd intended to shout came out as more of a cry. Looking down at myself, I saw I was covered in mud. "I will never be yours. Can't you see I belong here?"

A laugh mixed with a sob escaped me.

Still terrified, I knew I was meant to be at the bank of the river. The tree in front of me, the water flowing beside me, and the earth beneath me were my home.

Elle, I'm here. Kase's thoughts reached me. My head turned, not sure where I'd find him. He had to be close.

The surprise on my face alerted Marcel to my thoughts. I'd given Kase away. Marcel crouched down and surveyed the area.

On the other side of the tree. Kase couldn't read my mind, but it felt like he knew exactly what I was thinking.

My feet shuffled back a few steps, until Marcel spotted my

movement. He hissed at me, and I froze. The doorway between the roots was only a few feet away. I wasn't sure what would happen once I passed through, but my heart longed to find out. It was enough knowing Kase would be there waiting for me.

The sound of rock colliding with the mountainside echoed from above us. Marcel looked up, and I darted for the tree's protection. A white wolf, Joe, moved in on the scene, distracting Marcel while Kase stepped under the roots from the other side. Having Kase, my black wolf, at my side sent relief through me. It wasn't until Kase growled and flashed his canines that I realized we weren't out of danger.

"I hear they eat dog in other countries. I've never been curious what it tastes like until now." Anger oozed from Marcel's words when he glanced back at me to find Kase.

Marcel would have a fight on his hands with Kase and Joe, but I wouldn't underestimate his power. I had power of my own. Broadening my stance, I pressed my boots into the earth and spread my arms out. My fingertips touched the roots of the tree, and I reached outward for a source to connect with. Still weak, I hoped to meet the life source the roots were joined to, but something greater latched onto me.

Marcel's heightened abilities would eventually end in Kase's and Joe's deaths, and maybe my own. I had to protect us all. My heart longed for Kase and Joe to live, but it also yearned to protect this place from supernaturals who would abuse their power, or the power of the falls.

Unaware of how deep the tree's roots went or how far they reached, I called out with everything inside of me. I pleaded for help, not for myself, but for the mountain, my friends, and the falls. Magic tingled in my toes first, as if testing me. Power slowly made its way up my frame, and the surge filled me until it couldn't be held inside any longer. Flowing from beyond the tree's roots up into and through me, I accepted all of the magic and allowed it to use me as a vessel.

The strength of the stones making up the mountain made me feel indestructible. The speed of the water flowing in the river energized me. The awareness of the trees and the depth of the earth made me aware of everything and everyone around me.

I realized the amount of power made available to me could protect us all and that I hadn't merely bonded with the tree above me.

I'd bonded with the entire mountain.

Marcel lunged forward, rage etched on his face. A roar erupted from his lungs. Connecting to the mountain must have severed my blood bond to Marcel, or he would have been more careful before attacking me. Instinctively, I reached out with my power to a boulder. The giant rock lurched forward, groaning as it rolled in Marcel's direction. He leapt into the air over the boulder, avoiding what would have been a crushing weight. The near miss didn't rattle me, but Marcel's escape put him in closer proximity to Kase, who'd protectively bounded in front of me.

Marcel's eyes looked from me to the black wolf, and I didn't need to read his mind to know he had a new target. A low growl rumbled from Kase. The two stood facing off under a canopy of branches. I reached down, searching to communicate with the roots under me. The mountainside answered. One of the branches over Marcel popped and creaked, then broke loose. Marcel didn't have time to evade the attack, and the chunk of lumber struck him across his shoulders and knocked him to the ground.

An angry war cry erupted from Marcel as he pushed the branch to the side and laid eyes on me. He lunged with super speed, and I reacted by lifting one arm, summoning the waters to rise from the river. As I moved my hand in the air toward Marcel, a wave of water crashed into him.

Being swatted to the ground like a fly, Marcel had been knocked prostrate and soaked. He shook his head, and drops of water were flung in every direction. As he gathered his senses, his grimace slowly twisted into gaping awe. His eyebrows pulled together in fear. Marcel resembled a drowned rat, and when he twitched, I sensed he was about to run away.

My will communed with the mountainside, both reaching the same conclusion—Marcel must be stopped. The earth beneath me shook, and power vibrated in my chest. Both of my hands jutted forward, reaching out in front of me. The roots underground untangled and stretched up through the dirt to chase after and bind Marcel to the forest floor.

Thin leathery brown vines broke through the soil and wrapped themselves around Marcel's wrists and ankles. He bellowed in discomfort, laid out on his back, a wet, muddy mess. The trees around me waited for further instructions, and it blew my mind that I'd been entrusted with so much power. Kneeling down, I pressed my hands into the soil and said, "Thank you."

A bark sounded from behind me, and Kase nodded in the direction of the river. We had company. Joe was being followed by Willa, Scarlet, Tarron, Bale, Sheriff Kasun, and my parents. They all stood on the other side of the river, with a front-row view of what had just happened, each with their mouths hanging open.

CHAPTER 12

KASE

The Havenwood Falls High bell rang, signaling the end of the first school day back after spring break. My plan was to meet Elle after school and distract her long enough to carry out my epic promposal. She'd probably want to lose herself in a good book, but I needed to play to her adventurous side.

"Elle!" Calling out to her in public was usually something she hated, but today she turned to face me and smiled.

Over the last few days, with the help of her parents and friends, Elle had mostly figured out her new abilities, including a couple we hadn't expected. Her demonstration when releasing Marcel into my dad's custody was impressive. At one point, Marcel, roots still holding him, dangled ten feet in the air. I'd witnessed her power in the past, but we hadn't anticipated her control of water and rocks, or how she could sense things in the soil.

"What are you up to?" Her eyes narrowed suspiciously.

Focusing on anything but my plans, I answered, "I'm hoping to find out what you're up to. Want to hang out this afternoon?"

A few people looked our way when I took her hand. Students hustled around us in the hallway, and the latest gossip caught everyone's ears. Of course, Elle's kidnapping had remained a secret. The Court didn't like the idea of the supernatural community finding out a vampire made his way into town under false pretenses. They were under the impression Marcel arrived to vacation for the week. He left town with an official escort, and it was clear he'd never be welcome in Havenwood Falls again.

We discovered Mr. and Mrs. Martin boarded a flight on Thursday, after Mr. Martin explained to his wife that Marcel Cushing had been missing for two years. He hadn't told his wife or Elle about the Cushing family being excommunicated two years ago, because he thought Elle would blame herself.

"I'd love to do something. What are you thinking?" she asked me with furrowed brows. After I opened the door for her, Elle stepped outside. She waited for me to follow, then slid her hand up to my elbow and wrapped her arm around mine.

My chest filled with warmth. Giving up on Elle was never an option. I'd never stop loving her.

Elle Martin was everything I wanted in a girl. I just hadn't figured it out until she walked into my life. She was strong, confident, thoughtful, protective, and the most gorgeous woman I'd ever met. She paused mid-step and looked up at me with a smirk.

She caught me.

"Come on, Elle." My lips pulled together in embarrassment. "How about I take you out for coffee? I'll even throw in a scone."

The simplicity of my invitation was key. It couldn't imply anything more or she'd become suspicious.

Elle winked at me and said, "Why not? I'll take what I can get."

We walked to our cars, parked side by side at the back of the lot.

"Wanna ride together?" Driving my truck would be more comfortable.

"Are you offering to drive or ride?" she asked.

"Drive."

"Okay," she agreed with a shrug. So I reached for the handle of the passenger door. My dad and brothers had taught me to be a gentleman. I held a hand out for her backpack, and when she gave it to me, I tossed it into the back.

I started the truck and pulled out into the flow of traffic. A ton of the cars crossed Main Street and parked at Burger Bar for an "after school special." They thought they were pulling a fast one on us by calling the basket of fried food that, but Tate had filled me in on the teen dramas that used to be televised before I was born.

After maneuvering out of the parking lot, I relaxed a little. Getting to our destination after our friends was crucial. So I'd have to take the scenic route to Coffee Haven. I turned left on Fourth Street and waited for Elle to say something. Not one word came out of her mouth.

Taking a right on Blackstone Road, I could feel the curiosity bubbling inside her. She peered out the window, not looking my direction. When I turned right on Eleventh Street, Elle relaxed. We were headed toward the coffee shop again. The town square wasn't too busy, but I noticed my brother Conall in his patrol car in front of Backwoods. He was probably radioing Tate to warn them we were close.

Pulling into a space across the street from Coffee Haven, I kept the truck running, with the heat on, and unbuckled my seatbelt. "I know you're going to think I'm cheesy, but I'm thankful to have you in my life. I love you."

Shifting in her seat, Elle faced me and said, "I love you too."

"Remember when I promised to never hurt you?" I leaned closer to her and lifted my hand to her neck.

She nodded.

"I meant it, Elle." Reaching back behind my seat, I pulled out a white box—smaller than a shoe box and bigger than a jewelry box.

Elle's eyes widened, and her lips parted as she accepted it. "Do you want me to open it now?"

"Sure." My smile felt like it was going to split my cheeks.

She pulled the tape off and opened the lid. Beneath the tissue paper, a soft glow illuminated the inside of the box. Elle folded the thin paper back to reveal a white globe the size of my fist.

The moon had become a symbol of something more for us, and the night-light would always remind her of my promise. Capturing the moon was impossible, but I'd never give up on making Elle's dreams come true. She'd decided to stay in Havenwood Falls and take college courses online. While her parents were going to miss her, they supported her decision. Her mother understood on a personal level, and her father conceded after setting a few ground rules. Elle promised to finish college and pursue a career. She also agreed to visit New York once a quarter.

Elle pulled the globe out of the packaging, revealing a folded letter underneath. "What's this?"

"Read it." Even after everything that had happened in the last week, I knew she needed to read it.

She carefully unraveled the paper. It was plain printer paper, clearly printed from home, and Elle's head tilted when she recognized the logo, a purple square with a white torch at its center, at the bottom of the email. Elle's eyes swept over the first few lines, then she looked up at me.

"You've been accepted to NYU," she said, but her voice grew higher at the end like it was a question.

"Yeah."

She looked back at the paper, and wouldn't meet my eyes. "Are you leaving?"

Sliding my fingers to her chin, I lifted it. "Not unless you are. I wanted you to know that I'd planned to follow you to New York. I'd go anywhere with you."

Elle leaned forward and kissed me. Her lips searched mine, and I was tempted to forget the elaborate scheme I'd set in motion. Bale and Tarron had asked Scarlet and Willa to prom before spring break, so when I told them I wanted to ask Elle, they all insisted on helping.

Gently pulling away from Elle, I cleared my throat and said, "How about I start by following you into Coffee Haven?"

"Sounds like a plan, but what about this?" She smiled and waved the acceptance letter.

"I'll be taking classes online, and staying here to help with the store and patrolling."

Elle gave me a peck on the cheek, affirming my decision, and jumped out of the truck.

As we approached the coffee shop, I held my breath. Willa convinced me to let them handle most of the details because she was sure Elle would read my mind and figure everything out. This year's prom had a Wonderland theme, and I told Willa I wanted to ask Elle to prom during a tea party.

Before I could open the shop's door, Tarron bound out of it in a green top hat and jacket. He waved us inside, to one of the larger tables in the corner. Each of our friends wore some sort of costume. Willa sported a vest and pocket watch, Scarlet's cardigan was pink and purple stripes, and Bale had a yellow T-shirt on with a blue bowtie.

"Are you Tweedle Dum?" Elle asked Bale with a snicker.

"Don't push it," he warned. "I'm Tweedle Dee. I have an identical outfit for your boyfriend. He can be Tweedle Dum."

As hard as I tried to stay straight-faced, I couldn't, and neither could anyone else. We all started laughing. The teacup in front of Elle almost toppled over when she hit the table top with her hand. A teapot, with a card hanging from the handle, rattled. Willa had written *Open Me* on the card, and made similar decorative cards for the food and drink on the table.

We finally settled down, and Scarlet poured everyone tea while Tarron passed a plate of pastries. Elle reached for the lid of the teapot in front of her, and a string had been attached to the inside. She lifted and lifted, until the end of the string revealed two prom tickets. That was my cue.

Pulling a poster board out from under the table, I held it up for her to read. It said, *I wonder if you'll go to prom with me? Please, don't drive me mad, say yes!*

"Of course, yes," Elle said, so elated she hugged my neck.

It helped having a sister who could convince your buddies to dress up, but it was Tate who'd worked his magic with the markers. He'd always been the most creative of us all. And Conall probably worked out all the food and drinks. Then there was Elle. She lit up the room, and I was lucky to be close enough for her light to shine on me.

EPILOGUE

ELLE

Wonderland

*P*rom night had finally come. I'd been anticipating the dance for months, and the Havenwood Falls High School gymnasium had been transformed into Wonderland. Kase and I walked through a curtain of moss to find the gym transformed. Willa and Tarron walked in front of us, determined to find a table for the group. Folding chair surrounded life-sized mushrooms, for students to sit and eat at. The centerpieces were made up of toppling teapots. A chessboard had been set up at the center of the court for a dance floor, and an area beside the DJ booth was covered with green turf to play flamingo croquet.

Bale whistled from behind us, calling attention to the buffet tables. He and Scarlet went to grab snacks. Giant playing cards blocked off the bleachers, and the walls were covered in greenery and white roses sloppily painted red.

My own dress had been inspired by the roses. I wore a strapless white gown with a black floral print. The silver, glittering heels I wore had been a gift from my father—the actual surprise he had sent during spring break, not Marcel. They'd been delivered after my friends and I left for our camping trip. I'd thought about throwing them away, but they were too gorgeous to waste and went perfectly with my dress.

Kase had given me a wrist corsage made up of red roses. His tux was traditional black, and I'd pinned a red rose to his lapel. He looked more handsome in formal attire than I remembered.

Tarron and Willa waved us over to a table. Once we were all settled, and Bale had come back with thirds, Willa asked everyone about their favorite high school moments. We laughed about the time Tarron messed up Valentine's Day by persuading Ana Novak to be loving. Kase stayed quiet, but he didn't hold back his thoughts from me about missing Joe. His best friend had tracked me and Marcel and led Kase to us. Kase wanted to make it up to Joe and help him find Infiniti, if he could. Bale had us rolling when he started to try to explain who was who in our Scooby Gang. And then I asked everyone where they wanted to be in ten years.

The whole table fell silent. The beat of the music could be felt in the air, and the crowd's chatter had become white noise. I'd hoped the question would spark hope and maybe bring us closer together, but instead it created some unexpected space.

"Fine, I'll go first," I started, planting my elbows on the table. "In ten years, I still want to be friends with all of you."

I knew Willa was staying close to home for college, and Tarron was taking a gap year. Scarlet would be working at her family's store. When I glanced at Bale, he met my eyes and clenched his jaw.

"I want to be a mechanic," he blurted.

Everyone looked back and forth at each other, not sure how to respond. Scarlet even looked surprised. Kase was the first to find words.

"That's great, man. I'd trust my truck in your capable hands any day."

"Our truck," Willa corrected.

We all laughed, and before I could catch my breath, Kase scooted his chair back.

"Do you want to dance?" he asked and held his hand out.

"You know it." I took his hand and dragged him behind me to the checkered dance floor.

When we reached the center, Kase wrapped his arms around me. Above us, the Cheshire Cat sat on top of a spinning disco ball. Soon, Tarron and Willa, and Bale and Scarlet were dancing around us. The teen anthem faded into a classic, Mr. Moonlight. I looked up at Kase, and he smiled.

"How did you—"

Kase cut me off with a soft, lingering kiss, and it brought a smile to my face.

"I will always promise you the moon, Elle Martin."

We hope you enjoyed this story in the Havenwood Falls High series of novellas featuring a variety of supernatural creatures. The series is a collaborative effort by multiple authors.

Other Havenwood Falls by Kallie Ross about the Kasun Wolf Pack:

Written in the Stars
A Pack of Lies
Defying Gravity
Promise the Moon

You might also enjoy these other books in the Young Adult Havenwood Falls High series:

Bound by Shadows by Cameo Renae
Saving Infiniti by Rose Garcia
Cast in Moonlight by Ali Winters

Stay up to date at www.HavenwoodFalls.com

ABOUT THE AUTHOR

Writing unique adventures with heart.
 Kallie Ross has a passion for writing that has become an adventure in itself. She desires to create unique young adult fiction that incorporates legend, conjecture, fantasy, and conviction.

In addition to loving her life as a writer, Kallie adores being a wife, mother, friend, and teacher. She began her creative journey with books, a blog, a podcast, and lots of caffeine. Ross never imagined her own adventure would be filled with so many wonderful people or words!

KallieRoss.com
@KallieRoss {Instagram & Twitter}
Kallie Ross Books {Facebook}

ACKNOWLEDGMENTS

Thank you, Kristie Cook, for trusting me with the Kasuns. Kase and Elle are a story I've been thinking about since writing *Written in the Stars*. These two deserved to find love. I couldn't have finished this story without Morgan Wylie pushing me to write and holding me accountable. She is a wonderful friend and great writer. Go read her books!

Thank you, Rose Garcia, for letting me borrow Joe. Your patience with me, and love for Joe's story, made it possible for Kase and Elle to work out their story. All the Havenwood Falls authors are so supportive, and their input is always appreciated. Thanks to all of you.

Jessica Gibson was also a huge encouragement. I couldn't keep all my thoughts together without Jessi's help. She's my brainstorming buddy, as well as the one who keeps me calm when a deadline is looming.

My family is always supportive of my writing, and I am truly grateful for that blessing. Whether I'm hashing out an outline over breakfast or talking through a scene in the car line, my husband and kids always speak into my storytelling.

Lastly, I want to thank the Havenwood Falls readers. Your enthusiasm for this world keeps me dreaming up stories and writing them down. Thank you!

AN EXCERPT

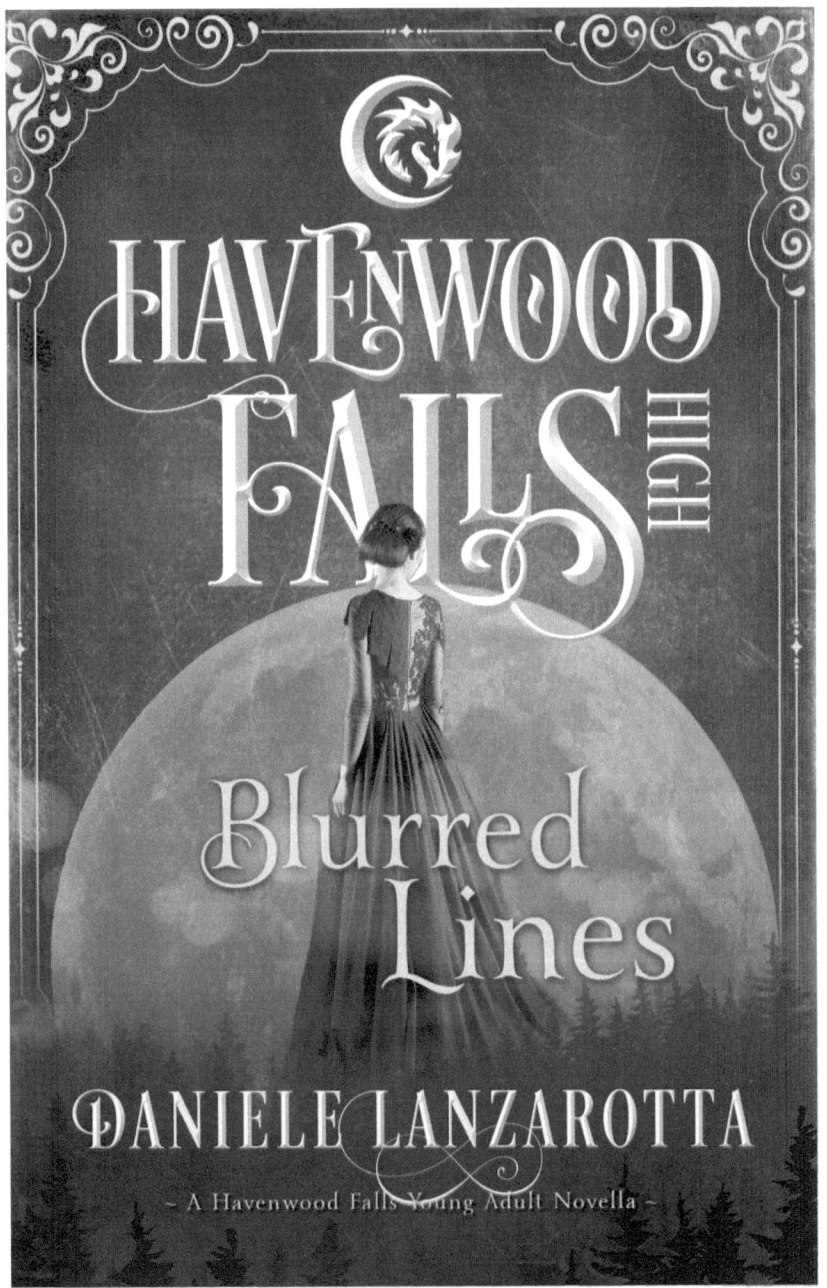

Blurred Lines (A Havenwood Falls High Novella) by Daniele Lanzarotta

After her brush with death, a young girl's humanity is at risk, and a guardian angel must choose between loving her and protecting her. Sequel to *Avenoir*.

Heidi Bennett's destiny was changed forever on the night of the Cold Moon Ball two winters ago. Months later, she was given a second chance at life—one that was supposed to restore life back to normal. Unfortunately for Heidi, things are not that simple.

The angels who know exactly what happened to her don't quite understand what she has become. Being able to read people's memories and learn secrets of many residents in Havenwood Falls is just one of the consequences. As time passes, Heidi distances herself more and more from the human she used to be, testing the boundaries of her new abilities. But when she's manipulated by a mysterious entity that controls her dreams, her behavior goes from reckless to downright dangerous.

With a desire to restore her humanity, guardian angel Zane becomes involved. Torn between his responsibilities as an angel and his love for Heidi, Zane has to decide between the two—but can he protect her if he turns his back on his own kind?

BLURRED LINES

BY DANIELE LANZAROTTA

ZANE

I sit on the roof at the house across the street from Heidi's and stare at her window from a distance. I've been sitting here for hours, and the open window has become this cruel joke. I can't stand knowing that she's right there, yet that I must stay away. Her lights are out, and the music is blasting. As much as I hate to admit it, I miss the pop songs she used to listen to. At least those had lyrics that could be understood. These new songs that she seems to like now sound like someone is screaming incoherently at you.

"Well, well." I hear a female's voice from behind me. I turn around to find Gabriella wearing a blue dress and high-heeled boots. She annoyingly taps her foot on the roof. Her arms are crossed, but she smiles when my eyes meet hers. "It's about time you decided to listen to me and check in on your girl. And thank you for clearing the snow off the roof this time."

I glare at Gabriella, the angel who has been keeping an eye on Heidi while I serve my punishment for bringing her back to life.

"She is not my girl," I say in a cold tone, to hide the fact that I wish more than anything that she could be.

Gabriella gives me a dramatic eye roll, then extends her hand.

"I need your jacket," she says. I take off my leather jacket and hand it to her. She lays it down and sits on top of it.

"Seriously?" I ask.

She shrugs. "It's not like you really need it. And I'd hate for my dress to get dirty."

"Yeah, because that seems like something you should be worried about," I say.

"Watch your tone, angel," she says jokingly. "I'm over here helping you out of the goodness of my heart, when I really shouldn't. You asked for help, and I volunteered to be her guardian angel, but I should be reporting all the stupid little things she has been pulling. Yet I'm keeping them a secret."

I look away and sigh.

"How is she?" I ask.

She chuckles. "Do you mean since the last update I gave you just a few days ago? When I begged you to come?"

Growing impatient, I just shake my head. "It's not exactly easy for me to leave without them knowing. They think I'm watching over someone else right now." I pause. "Now can you please just stop torturing me and answer the question?" I beg.

"Such a funny request coming from someone who is known to be incapable of giving straight answers," she says in a sarcastic tone.

I glare at her.

Gabriella puts her hands up. "Fine . . . fine. She's not doing any better. She's not herself. She's lonely. She skips school. She wanders around in the woods. The list goes on and on . . . and there is not much I can do without breaking rules to intervene with her life."

I sigh. I used to hate watching Heidi and Jace together. Since they have broken up, I hate the fact that she's alone even more. At least he was good for her. He was helping her heal in ways I cannot.

"I'm sure she's just acting out," I say. "She and Jace aren't together. I'm certain she's just sad, depressed—whatever human reaction is normal in those cases. She'll come around."

"Argh." Gabriella lets out a frustrated growl. "And that is exactly why I begged you to come back—so you can see it for yourself."

I open my mouth to argue with her, but she cuts me off.

"And yes, she is lonely. She barely talks to anyone, but that and her other behaviors can't possibly be for breaking up with someone she fell out of love with."

I lean my head down. "How do you know she fell out of love with him?"

Gabriella pauses, but I keep my head down. I'm afraid to hear her answer out loud.

"You know," she says, "for someone who has been around for so many decades, you sure are dense." Her tone grows frustrated.

I look up and stare at Heidi's window again.

"She's not home, by the way," she finally says.

"Where is she? Why aren't you watching her?" I growl.

She chuckles. "Let's say she has become an expert at escaping." She nods toward the window. "The lights out and music thing seems mostly to fool her parents. They think she's sleeping. I followed her all the way to her dad's market on Miller's Plaza. She probably knew I was near. She left through the back door without me noticing. We both know we lost the ability to track her, so I decided to just come straight here and wait."

I stand up, agitated, and start to pace back and forth on the roof. "Any idea where we should look? Where has she been going lately?"

She shrugs. "You could go to the library and look for her. I know she liked spending time there. Or you can sit and wait. She'll come back home eventually. She always does."

HEIDI

I sit at the dinner table, staring at my plate as Mom lectures me about missing school. This is our new routine. As Mom goes on and on about being disappointed, Dad gets lost in a memory of us eating a peaceful dinner together just a little over a year ago. I was excitedly telling them about my day at school and then about my dance recital's costume. He misses how things used to be. I know that, logically, I should too. But I feel nothing.

That was before I was killed. December 2, 2018, was the night I disappeared. Hurt by some screwed up angel, I ended up in a coma and died months later. Another angel, Zane, brought me back to life, and somehow, I came back with a special ability to read people's memories. If Mom and Dad only knew . . . Like most, they believe I have no recollection of what really happened to me. They just know that I went missing and eventually found my way back. I wonder if things would be less awful for them if they knew that this curse to pick up on people's memories is what destroyed so many things I used to love. I can see every single detail of a memory with such clarity, it is as if I were there at the moment when it happened. Some days—well, most days—I just need a break.

"I'm going to bed," I tell Mom in the middle of her sentence. She just sighs and throws her napkin down on the table. I can tell she's on the verge of giving up on me. I can't believe she hasn't already.

Without looking back, I rush upstairs and slam my door shut. I turn the music on and pace back and forth. This music tends to numb my thoughts in a way, but tonight, nothing seems to be helping. I feel like I'm all over the place. I feel irritable about . . . well, everything.

"I need to get out of here," I say out loud.

I put on a dark hoodie and coat and walk out of my room, locking the door from the inside and putting a hair clip in my pocket so I can get back in later. If Mom and Dad come to check on me, they'll think I'm doing homework or that I fell asleep. I quietly make my way downstairs. I hear them talking in the kitchen, so I go the other way, grabbing Dad's store keys on the way out.

I curse myself for not waiting until later to leave. I have come to love nighttime, when there is barely anyone out. Right now, the streets have more people than I care to see. I avoid going anywhere near Town Square to get to Miller's Plaza, but even the back roads have a few tourists walking around and admiring the small-town charm and stunning mountain views. I roll my eyes at the sound of that. You'd think after a day of skiing, they would be tired and want to lock themselves in their rooms.

I freeze in place when I see a family of four walking around. The parents carry the two little boys. Based on their memories, I can tell they are visiting from Italy. *If they only knew they're putting their kids in danger just by walking around at night,* I think to myself. Anger consumes me as I start to wonder how many of these tourists will actually make it back home after vising here.

I decide to approach the couple.

"Excuse me," I say. The young couple stops walking and looks at me with smiles on their faces, even though they look tired. There is no telling how long they've been walking around carrying their kids in the snow.

"Hello," they say.

I smile back. There is no easy way to tell them this. I look at my watch. "Are you heading back to where you are staying? It's not too safe to be out at this time of night."

Well, that didn't sound creepy at all.

"But you are out," the man says in a heavy accent.

I take a deep breath and try not to sound rude. "Well, yes, but I live right here," I tell them. "And I know what I am talking about. It's not safe."

Yep. They think I'm crazy. I can tell by the nonchalant look in their eyes.

"Thank you," they say and start to walk again.

I sigh. It's not like they would have believed me if I told them there are vampires roaming around—among other things.

I keep walking west, and once I get to Miller's Plaza, I absentmindedly stop in front of the dance studio I used to love. I zone out for a while. It's the feeling of my fingernails digging into my skin that brings me back to the here and now. I turn around and keep walking toward my dad's market.

Once in the market, I welcome the quiet of being here after hours —when the store is free of people walking around. Thankful for Dad being in the midst of switching security systems, I take my time walking down every aisle, even though I know what I'm here for. When I get to the aisle with hair products, I stop and stare at the variety of options. I grab the darkest one I can find. *Perfect.* I need a change, and this is fitting. I make my way to the back of the store. Dad bought a machine to make T-shirt designs shortly after he bought the store, so he can make some extra cash during the many town events and fundraisers. From that day, I started to design my own collection of shirts. I grin at the thought of people's reactions when I start wearing them.

As the first one is printing, I grab a bag of chips and a can of soda from the office. I sit down and reach for the can first.

"Ouch." I feel the small piece of metal piercing through my skin as I open the can. It's a small scratch, but enough to cut through my skin. I watch it as it quickly heals right before my eyes. This happened once before with a paper cut, and it healed just as fast. I stare at my finger for long after it is healed. *Maybe I should be happy about this.* I chuckle. *Happy—I can't even remember what that feels like.* Either way, this just opens up a whole new set of questions—like what the hell am I? I see my parents' memories. They miss the cheerful, sweet, nice daughter I once was. Not the distant, alone, cold version of her that they have today.

"Ugh. Snap out of it, Heidi," I tell myself. I open the bag of chips and start eating it.

I spend the next half hour or so enjoying my peace and quiet, until I get a text from Ani Rukska, the witch who made it possible that I no longer pick up on Jace's memories, and the only person whom I've told the truth about my abilities.

Ani: I'm by the back door of the store. We need to talk.

I roll my eyes and contemplate just ignoring her message, but unfortunately, that doesn't mean she will go away.

I hop off the office chair and let her in.

She closes the door behind her, and I cross my arms over my chest.

"How did you know I was here after hours?" I ask.

She grins. "Location spell," she says proudly. She pauses. "By the way, someone followed you here."

Of course, I think to myself. That is the angel Zane has following me around. I can't pick up on her memories to know when she's around, but luckily, she doesn't care to hide the fact that I'm being watched.

"I'm aware," I say. "Female, long hair, dark skin, extremely well dressed?" I ask in an annoyed tone.

"Yep. That would be the one."

"So . . . Do you want to go somewhere else and talk?" I ask.

She nods. "That would be best. Let's go to my house."

"Just give me a few minutes," I say. I turn off the machine and grab the first few shirts and the bag with hair dye. I throw the drink and bag of chips out, but leave the lights on so the angel thinks I'm still here. Dad will probably just think that he forgot to turn it off anyway. We get out through the back door, and I follow Ani to her house.

When we are some distance away from the store, she chuckles. "What?" I ask.

"I'm guessing you escaped from her before?" she asks.

I shrug. "Wouldn't you have? I don't particularly like being followed." I pause. "Or found through location spells," I snap.

She smirks. "Something is different about you. Sneaking out, being out this late, snappy comments," she says. "I like it."

I roll my eyes at her. "I'm sure you do."

We continue the walk in silence. At some point, I hear howling in the distance, but those sounds don't even faze me anymore. I find it amusing that Ani watches me to see if I react at all. She doesn't say anything when she realizes that I don't. When we get to her house, I walk in after her.

A part of me expected to walk in and find potions and such all over the place, but her house is actually normal. No one would even be able to tell that she is what she is.

"So, what is it that you wanted to talk about?" I ask.

"Have a seat," she says. "Do you want something to drink?"

"I'm good. Thanks," I say in a cold tone. *Who in their right mind would accept a drink from a witch?*

"Okay, then," she says as she sits down. I remain standing. "I'll get right to it so you can get home. I'd like to collect on the favor you owe me."

"Go on," I tell her.

She hands me a piece of paper with five names. I read over them: Michaela Petran, Mathilde Augustine, Lilith Blackstone, Lawrence Mills, and Roman Bishop. I chuckle at the last name, as I already know a few of his secrets. I fold the list and look at Ani.

"I'd like to know everything you can get on their memories," she says.

I grin at her.

"Why would I do that?" I ask as I tilt my head to the side.

"Because you owe me," she says in an awkward tone.

I sigh. "Now, see . . . we have a difference in opinions about that. I came to you and asked you to keep me from reading memories in general and to forget a certain someone. All you did was block Jace's memories for me."

She stands up and closes the distance between us. She tries to look collected, but I can tell she's in shock. My grin widens.

"You're playing with fire, child."

"Am I?" I ask her.

She nods. Once. "I can just as easily undo that spell."

I shrug. "We have broken up since then. What's one more person's memories to pick up on?" I smile at her.

"I could tell your secret," she says.

I laugh. "You could. But then again, I have this list you just gave me. I'm sure you wouldn't want these people knowing of your interest in their memories—or that you knew about me and have been hiding my secret for your own selfish reasons."

She gapes.

I chuckle. "I guess I should let myself out," I say, turning around to leave.

"You don't know who you are messing with, little girl," she warns as I open the door.

"Uh huh," I say before heading home.

Purchase **Blurred Lines** where books are sold.

www.ingramcontent.com/pod-product-compliance
Lightning Source LLC
Chambersburg PA
CBHW052008170626
46808CB00007B/2832